Lucy Willow

Lucy

Willow

Sally Gardner

Illustrated by Peter Bailey

Orion
Children's Books

First published in Great Britain in 2006
by Orion Children's Books
a division of the Orion Publishing Group Ltd
5 Upper St Martin's Lane
London WC2H 9EA

Text © Sally Gardner 2006
Illustrations © Peter Bailey 2006

A catalogue record for this book is
available from the British Library.

ISBN-10: 1 84255 532 4
ISBN-13: 978 1 84255 532 3

Printed and bound in Great Britain by
Clays Ltd, St Ives plc.

The Orion Publishing Group's policy is to use papers that
are natural, renewable and recyclable products and made
from wood grown in sustainable forests. The logging and
manufacturing processes are expected to conform to the
environmental regulations of the country of origin.

www.orionbooks.co.uk

To my sister Lucy,
with all my love

Contents

I

Three Things About Lucy Willow

There were three things that marked out Lucy Willow as different from other children.

The first was that she lived on a train.

The second, just as important, was that she had a snail called Ernest as a pet.

And the third, the most important of all, was that she had green fingers. That means that she had a gift for growing things, though at the time this story begins she didn't know it.

The Willow family hadn't always lived on a train. When Lucy was younger they had lived in London, on the seventeenth floor of a high-rise block of flats. Dad didn't like heights, they made him feel sick. Mum too felt a little

queasy and just wanted a place of their own in the country. This was no good for Dad, who worked in the City. They couldn't agree what to do for the best, though they both knew that something had to be done.

Mum dreamed of having a garden for vegetables and flowers. Up there in the clouds was no place for plants. Every month she would buy magazines full of pictures of country cottages, lovingly restored.

'Ah,' Mum would sigh. 'That's my kind of house.'

If you had asked Dad what kind of house he dreamed of, without a doubt he would have said an old railway station. A converted

2

signal box, maybe. For his passion was trains. His favourites were old steam trains. To him, they were as wonderful as dragons. He loved the noise they made and the way they blew steam out of their funnels, their colours, their names, and their numbers. Oh, I think it might be better to stop there. Once you got Mr Willow on to the subject of steam trains, there was no knowing where it would end.

But what about Lucy Willow, with her chocolate brown eyes and her pretty dimples that showed every time she smiled? Where did she want to live? Why, that was easy. She didn't mind as long as they were all happy. She did have responsibilities, though. She had her pet snail, Ernest, whom she kept in a shoebox and who went everywhere with her. Lucy thought a bit of greenery would be good for his constitution.

'Snails,' said Lucy, 'like being on the ground near nature. They aren't made for living on the seventeenth floor with the pigeons.'

As it turned out, it was Dad's love of trains that would hold the answer to all their problems. One Saturday morning, while flicking through his train magazines, he saw an advertisement. It said simply:

A HOME FOR SALE

3 bedrooms, bathroom, kitchen/dining room
and must-see sitting room

'Why,' said Mum, 'it's just what we need.'

'It's a bing-bang bargain,' said Dad.

'Well then,' said Mum, 'what are we waiting for?'

'There is just one small thing,' said Dad.

'What's that?' asked Mum.

'The house is made up from three carriages.'

'I can deal with that,' said Mum.

'There is just one other teeny-weeny hitch,' said Dad.

'What's that?' asked Mum.

'The carriages are still attached
to the train.'

'Oh,' said Mum.

'But the good
thing about it,'
said Dad, 'is that

the train goes backwards and forwards
between Liverpool Street Station and Maldon-
in-the-Marsh.'

'Where's that?' asked Mum.

Dad smiled. This was his trump card. 'A
pretty country village.'

'All right,' said Mum, still a little unsure.
'Why does it go there?'

'Aha!' said Dad with pride. 'Because this is
the last steam train to run to any village. A Mr
Opal owns the train. He's something in
confectionery. Anyway, to cut a long story
short, his old mum lives in Maldon-in-the-
Marsh and she has never been too keen on all
these new-fangled trains. Likes steam best. A
lady after my own heart.'

Mum gave Dad's suggestion some thought.
Then she said, 'Well, you work in the City and

we have always wanted to live in the country and this, I suppose, is the best of both worlds. After all, beggars can't be choosers.'

You have to take your hat off to Mum; she was always good at looking on the bright side.

That settled it. They said goodbye to the flat and moved into their new home. Ever since then, they had been shunted up and down from London to the country and back again Mondays to Saturdays every week. Well, maybe a little less when you take into account holidays, snow, leaves on the line, and once even the great excitement of a fallen tree.

2
The Train

It was an unusual place to live. The three carriages that made up their home had been sold with fixtures and fittings, which looked faded and very grand.

The first carriage had been made into a kitchen. Mum hung pretty curtains at the windows and kept her pans in the luggage rack.

The second carriage had a corridor running all along the carriage with rooms off to one side. There were two bedrooms and a bathroom, each with its own sliding door.

The third carriage was divided up into a master bedroom and next to that a grand sitting room with a real wow factor to it. It was this carriage that had won Mum over to the idea of living on a train. There were gilded mirrors and a real chandelier that jingled and

jangled as the train click-clacked along, and a
buttoned velvet sofa that felt prickly on the
bottom when you
sat down, as if it
had been stuffed
with the wrong
end of the
feathers. At the
end of the room
there were doors
with patterned
frosted glass that
opened on to a
balcony, where on
fine days the
Willows would

sit, watching where they had just come from
disappear into the distance.

There was much that Lucy liked about living
on the train. On winter evenings, she loved
looking out of her bedroom window at all the
people huddled on the platforms waiting for

their trains, fed up with journeys, dreaming of home, while she lay snug as a bug in a rug in her nice warm bed enjoying being rocked to sleep by the movement of the train. It made her feel safe to think that the  driver and the guard were awake and working while she was in the land of dreams . . .

The only drawback to being attached to a train that went between Liverpool Street Station and Maldon-in-the-Marsh was that their lives were run by train timetables. And as we all know, timetables are a law unto themselves. It was the train timetables that decided where Lucy went to school. There was no choice.

The train arrived at Liverpool Street at 6.16

in the morning, just in time for Dad to get to his office in the City. Then it shunted off again towards Maldon-in-the-Marsh, arriving there at 8.24, just in time for Lucy to walk to the village school. At 4.30 the train doors would shut and the train huffed and puffed its way out of the station back towards Liverpool Street.

Dad would join the train at 6.29 after finishing work in time for Lucy's tea, bath and bedtime. Then, at 8.30 on the dot, the whistle would blow once again and the train would steam out of Liverpool Street, stopping at all the small forgotten stations, delivering the mail up and down the line throughout the night and arriving back at Liverpool Street just in time for Dad to go to work.

So you can see that trains and timetables ruled the Willows' lives, and Lucy was sure that this was the way their world would spin forever.

Then suddenly, and for no good reason Lucy could think of, her mum and dad announced, as if it was the best news ever, that Lucy was going to have a baby brother or sister.

'Isn't it wonderful?' said Dad, looking as chuffed as if he had just won the lottery.

'Well, no, not really,' said Lucy. 'Why would I want a brother or sister, for pity's sake, when I am practically all grown-up?'

Mum said kindly that she would get used to the idea and in the end be as pleased as they were, which Lucy knew was just plain silly. What is wrong with grown-ups? she thought miserably. Why do they never listen?

Mum went into labour in the middle of the night. The driver shunted the train backwards as far as it could go so that she could get to a maternity hospital. And would you believe it? They didn't make it on time. Typical! Zac was born on the train while Lucy was asleep. They could at least have woken her.

The baby confirmed what Lucy already

knew, which was that babies were very over-rated and if Stench, as she called him, was anything to go by, a complete waste of time.

'How old does my baby brother have to be before he can play with me?' she asked. And on being told, she said grumpily, 'Why did you bother?'

Babies, unlike trains, don't run to timetables and Mum got all flustered and stressed. Especially after Dad said that he could not take time off from his job. There was a crisis in the office, and all the staff were expected to work round the clock to save the business.

Mum was left trying to sort out the baby and the shopping, keep the train tidy and cook meals. There was so much washing that needed to be done that buckets with Stench's smelly nappies were forever being forgotten, only to fall over when the train began to move. It was enough to put a girl off her cornflakes.

Dad was hardly ever there these days. The train just click-clacked back and forth without him, to the sound of Stench's crying. No, things were not going well.

Then one Wednesday, a day that always makes you think the weekend is too far away for its own good, Lucy got home from school to find Dad sitting at the kitchen table in his suit, his tie undone, looking pale and worried.

'You shouldn't be here,' said Lucy, giving him a big hug. 'We don't pick you up until 6.29.'

He nodded sadly. 'Yep, I know,' he said. 'That's how things used to run.'

'Is everything all right?' asked Lucy. She

looked around the kitchen, pleased to see that Stench was fast asleep in his cot.

'I've been made redundant,' said Dad.

'What does that mean?' asked Lucy.

'It means that I've lost my job,' replied Dad.

'Oh George,' said Mum, 'I'm sure something will turn up.'

3

The End of the Line

'All Change' was the name Lucy had given Maldon-in-the-Marsh. She would hear the stationmaster shout it out every time they arrived.

'This train,' he would bellow, 'has reached the end of the line. All change.'

As the weeks went by and Dad hadn't found another job, those words began to have a worrying ring.

'How are we going to pay the mortgage?' asked Dad. 'My savings are nearly spent, and the bank won't lend us another penny.'

'That's ridiculous,' said Mum.

'Train carriages are not what they call a sound investment,' said Dad gloomily.

Lucy heard these alarming conversations as she lay in bed thinking and wondering what on earth would happen next.

What happened next began on the day
Stench's first tooth appeared and he was
screaming at full blast.

A brown envelope came through their
letterbox. It said that Mr Opal was
sorry to report that his
mother had passed
away and there was
no more need for him
to keep the train
running. Therefore, he
had sold the line and the
stock to Bridgemount Railway Company. He
hoped they would keep things just the way
they were.

Mr Willow
Railway Carriages
Maldon in the Marsh
ENGLAND

The next day a notice was stuck to the door
of the front carriage. It said that Bridgemount
Railway Company had been taken over by a
Texan billionaire, a Mr Buzz Logan, who had
plans to develop the line. It went on to say the
company was committed to the safety of the
general public and was not a housing
association. A telephone helpline number
followed.

'What does that mean?' asked Mum above the noise of Stench's crying.

'I wish I knew,' said Dad.

He spent the rest of the day on the phone trying to get through to someone. Finally he spoke to a very nice gentleman in Delhi who said he was very sorry but he could not help. He suggested writing or e-mailing the new owner.

'What are we going to do, George?' asked Mum looking tearful, which was very unlike her.

'I suppose someone will tell us what's going on,' said Dad.

'Will we have to move?' asked Lucy.

'I don't know. We own the carriages but without somewhere for them to go we are pretty stuck,' said Dad.

'It's not looking good,' said Lucy to Ernest, who for a snail was a very good listener. 'What happens if we're left in a siding near Liverpool Street Station? How would I get to school then?'

Ernest stuck out his long eyes and looked pretty shocked at the idea of being abandoned

 in a grubby old siding
with not a plant in
sight.

'I know,' said Lucy.
'Things are bad.'

Ernest looked as if he
might be saying, 'If only
humans carried their homes on their backs like
me,' which Lucy thought was a bit irritating as
they were all in this mess together, shell or no
shell.

A week later a very smart man turned up at
Liverpool Street Station. He knocked on their
front door and introduced himself as Mr
Dallas. He said he was here on behalf of Mr
Buzz Logan. Mum and Dad took him into the
kitchen.

Mr Dallas looked around. 'You have made a
mighty fine home here, if I may say so,
ma'am,' he said in a long-drawn-out Texan
accent.

'Thank you,' said Mum. She made a pot of

tea while Dad sat nibbling his nails in a nervous kind of way.

Mr Dallas took out a laptop from his briefcase. It made a heavy bong as the screen flashed into life.

'Let's get straight to the point,' said Mr Dallas. 'After all, time is money and money is time. The bottom line is this, you own these three carriages and we own the track.'

'That's right,' said Dad. 'We bought — '

'The problem,' interrupted Mr Dallas sharply, 'is that we don't want your carriages on our tracks any more. Not the right image for the twenty-first century. You get my point.'

'But you can't do that. It's the oldest steam train in the country, and the only one that's still running. It's historic,' said Dad.

'It's history,' said Mr Dallas firmly. 'We are

looking toward the future, not the past. That was yesterday. We are about tomorrow.'

'So what are we supposed to do today?' asked Mum.

'Find yourself some land that you can put your carriages on,' said Mr Dallas.

'But,' said Dad, 'that will cost a fortune and we don't have a fortune.'

'Buts are for babies, Mr Willow,' snapped Mr Dallas.

Right on cue Stench started to scream. You could see that Mr Dallas didn't like babies. 'Does that infant have a volume control?' he asked. 'If it does, could you turn it down?'

'No he doesn't,' said Mum. 'Please, can you tell us just what's going to happen?'

'A pleasure, ma'am,' said Mr Dallas, putting his laptop back into the briefcase. You could see that he was keen to be gone. 'Mr Logan is a family man and out of the kindness of his heart he is going to give you three months to make alternative arrangements. For the time being you will be shunted into a siding at Maldon-in-the-Marsh and we will, for a small fee, supply you with water, electricity and plumbing. Mr Logan will charge you a rent for the site. When the three months are up we will expect you to have the train moved from the siding.'

'That will need a crane,' said Dad. 'Have you any idea how much that will cost?'

'In the thousands,' said Mr Dallas, without a blink of the eye. He handed them the breakdown of the rent for the three-month period.

Mum and Dad stared at the figures put in front of them.

'This is daylight robbery,' said Dad.

'No,' said Mr Dallas. 'This is Mr Logan being generous. Take it or leave it.'

Dad had no option. He took it.

'One last thing,' said Mr Dallas, snapping shut his briefcase. 'If these carriages aren't gone in three months, we will have your home taken away for scrap.'

'You can't do that,' said Dad.

'With a billion pounds in the bank Mr Logan can do what he damn well pleases,' said Mr Dallas as he left the train.

That evening they shunted out of Liverpool Street Station for the last time. At Maldon-in-the-Marsh the carriages were uncoupled from the train and the Willow family watched sadly as it puffed and click-clacked its way back to London and retirement without them.

'Well,' said Mum, walking Stench up and down, 'being still might do us a lot of good. The country air will help Zac sleep.'

'I can't believe they've done this,' said Dad as he looked out over the meadows on one side of the carriage and a stream on the other side. 'It's a crime, I tell you. We have arrived in the middle of nowhere, and there's hardly any time to sort this pickle out.'

'We're not quite in the middle of nowhere. We're at Maldon-in-the-Marsh and Lucy's school,' said Mum, trying her best to sound encouraging.

'True,' said Dad. 'What do you think, Lucy?'

'We won't let that horrid man take our house, will we?' asked Lucy.

'Not if I can help it,' said Dad. 'We will get out of this mess if it's the last thing I do.'

'Oh George,' said Mum, 'that's the spirit.'

'I suppose,' said Lucy, 'it could be loads worse. We could have ended up in a siding near Liverpool Street Station. Then how would I have got to school, for pity's sake?'

'Come here, Lucy,' said Mum, and she gave

her a great big hug.

'Anyway,' said Lucy, enjoying feeling important, 'it's about time Dad pulled his socks up around the house instead of always sloping off to work.'

Mum and Dad burst out laughing, though what was so funny Lucy couldn't work out. Grown-ups, she thought, were a complete mystery.

Lucy lay in bed that night and thought of all the things she would now be able to do. She could go to her friends' houses without worrying about missing the train. Friends could come back to her house without the problem of ending up at Liverpool Street Station.

'Yes,' said Lucy to Ernest sleepily, 'I think this is going to be all right.'

Ernest said nothing, for he was tucked up safe and sound in his shell.

A snail, you know, needs his beauty sleep.

4
A Bit Behind with the Planting

The next day Lucy took Ernest to school for show and tell. That's where you show something off that you like, then tell the class about it.

Lucy stood up that morning near her teacher's desk and told everyone her news. Miss Robinson was pleased to hear that their train had come to the end of the line at last, and so were all her friends, especially Mindy Moxon and Tom Cole, Lucy's two best friends in the whole wide world.

Then she showed them Ernest. She had wanted to do this for a long time but had been too worried about forgetting him and being unable to go back for him on account of missing the train. Now she was still, he could come to school with her every day without

Show and tell

fear of being left behind.

For some strange reason that Lucy couldn't work out, half the class didn't seem too keen on Ernest.

'Ugh, that's too gross,' they said.

'It isn't,' said Lucy. 'It's just Ernest leaving a slimy silver trail behind him. He is a snail after all, for pity's sake.'

Miss Robinson thought Ernest looked a very handsome and well-cared-for snail.

Lucy liked Miss Robinson. She was a nice, chubby lady with glasses, which seemed to spend most of their time playing hide and seek with her. She was always in a muddle and a bit given to flapping and wore red quite a lot.

'Today we are going to grow sunflowers,' said Miss Robinson, looking flustered. 'I'm afraid we might have left it a bit late. Mrs Sparks's class planted theirs about a month ago.'

A groan went up from the class.

Mrs Sparks was the head teacher. None of the children liked her and all the staff seemed scared of her.

Mrs Sparks was tall and thin and sharp, like a pencil, and spoke with a stuck-on accent. Mindy said she was sure she was a witch because of her long red fingernails. Tom thought the fact that she had four eyes didn't help. Her hair looked like a helmet, all backcombed, and the fringe was curled at the front so she looked as if she had strange frog eyes on top of her head. She was always perfectly dressed, with a brand-new outfit for every day of the week.

It was Mrs Sparks who had insisted on school uniform, which could only be bought at one shop in Maldon-in-the-Marsh. It cost so much money that Dad and Mum wondered if they could afford to send Lucy there. A few children from the village had had to leave, the uniform being too much for the family budget, and they now had to travel miles to another school halfway across the county; it had caused an outcry at the time and there had been a bit about it in the local paper. Mrs Sparks had written a robust reply saying that bad education came from sloppy dressing and that all her children looked smart and acted smart. Nothing more was said.

Mrs Sparks had also raised the price of school dinners and refused to let any children bring in lunchboxes. As she said to the parents, 'A school that eats together stays together.' The dinners now cost twice as much and were three times as bad.

No, Lucy and the rest of the pupils didn't like Mrs Sparks, with her airs and graces for the parents, and shouts and slaps for the children.

It was a bit of a blow, then, to know that her class of ten handpicked pupils had planted their sunflowers so long ago. Lucy had seen the earthenware pots sitting on the windowsill, with healthy shoots showing.

Miss Robinson's class of thirty were each given a small plastic cup filled with a bag of

earth and an envelope with a seed in it. Some
with great care and some with less put the
earth in the pot. They pushed their sunflower
seeds into the soil and watered them. Then
they all washed their hands and stood and
admired thirty pots with their names stuck on.

Mindy said that she was very good at
growing cress on a clay sheep.

'Why on a clay sheep?' asked Lucy.

'Because it looks like green wool and Mum
likes to eat it,' said Mindy.

Lucy was none the wiser for knowing that.

Tom's father had a farm and they grew all
sorts of things, so Tom said that growing things
was no big deal.

However, when Lucy put her seed in her pot

she had the most odd feeling. A
tingling of the fingertips.

'Good heavens, Miss
Robinson,' said Mrs Sparks
when she popped her head
round the classroom door and
saw the pots of earth. 'Why
have you left the planting

until so late? You know perfectly well that I want the school to put on a good show for the Governors' Competition.'

'Nobody told me we were going in for a competition,' said Miss Robinson.

'Well, we are,' said Mrs Sparks. 'The Governors are awarding a cash prize for the winner. My class is coming along very well. Yours, I'm afraid, is letting the school down as usual.' And with that she marched out, the door slamming shut behind her.

'Oh dear,' said Miss Robinson. 'I don't know what we can do to catch up.'

What neither Mrs Sparks nor Miss Robinson had counted on was Lucy Willow, and what that strange tingling feeling in her fingers might mean.

5

Guess What?

The next day Lucy couldn't wait to get to school to see how her sunflower was doing.

'How long do sunflowers take to grow?' she asked her mum at breakfast.

Mum was feeding Stench and had that half-listening look in her eyes. 'Ages,' she said.

That disappointed Lucy a lot, for she didn't want Mrs Sparks to be right. She tried to ask more questions about sunflowers as Mum pushed the pram to school and Stench screamed until he fell asleep, but it was no good. He really is a waste of time, thought Lucy. He sleeps all day and screams all night and then when he smiles, Mum and Dad look as if he has just scored a goal for England. I don't get a look-in.

As Lucy waved goodbye to Mum she saw Tom in the playground.

'Guess what?' he said, rushing up to her. 'Silverboots McCoy is getting married!'

'Who to?' asked Lucy.

'Give a guess.'

That was what Tom always said to everything, 'Give a guess.'

'I haven't a clue,' said Lucy.

Mindy came running up waving a newspaper cutting.

'Blossom B is going to marry Silverboots McCoy! I love Blossom B,' said Mindy. 'I've got all her music on my iPod.'

'Wow! What would I give to have a look inside his house,' said Lucy.

Now I should say, just in case you don't know, that Silverboots McCoy was the golden boy of football and Maldon-in-the-Marsh's one and only famous resident. It was he who had given the money for a new sports hall for the school, all glass and sparkle. He owned a mansion just outside the village. It had very high brick walls and large electronically controlled gates. No one knew what it was like inside.

Mindy was sure there was an Olympic-sized swimming pool and a Jacuzzi in the bedroom.

'I bet they have a gym and a tennis court,' said Lucy.

'And a proper football pitch where Silverboots can practise,' said Tom.

Just then Miss Robinson rang the bell so they had to go into school. The news was so exciting that all the children whispered through Assembly, talked about it through PE and continued all through the lunch break.

The only thing that made Lucy, Mindy and

34

Tom go quiet was the sight of
thirty little plastic cups on
the Nature Table with nothing
in them but earth. All except
for one, and the name on that
pot was Lucy Willow. The
little plastic pot had split
right down the side, and the
sunflower needed re-potting

pretty quickly. Miss Robinson stared at it.

'My word, Lucy,' she said. 'Who would have
thought it! You must have green fingers.'

Lucy nodded in agreement, mainly because
everyone in the class was looking at her. She
hadn't a clue what Miss Robinson meant by
green fingers, so instead she just said, 'I know,'
in a very grown-up way.

'What did you do to it?' asked Mindy,
looking gloomily at her plastic cup, which had
nothing, not even the smallest shoot, showing.

'Green fingers, and Ernest I think,' said
Lucy, for his shoebox was standing next to her
pot.

The sunflower was re-potted with more

earth, this time in a plastic flowerpot. Lucy carefully put it on the class windowsill so that it could see the sun and wouldn't feel lonely.

English was taken that day in Mrs Sparks's class with her top ten handpicked girls, who were allowed to sit in chairs while Lucy's class sat cross-legged on the floor.

Today Mrs Sparks looked even more pleased with herself than usual. She was wearing a bright pink suit and a huge amount of really stinky perfume which made you long to open a window.

'If she wore any more make-up she'd look like a clown,' whispered Mindy.

Lucy tried not to giggle, for if Mrs Sparks caught her there would be
trouble. She was known to have a terrible tornado of a temper.

Once a boy called Arnold Jones had interrupted and Mrs Sparks was so angry that she had dragged him to his feet and torn the arms of his school blazer. Then she coolly told his parents that he wouldn't be allowed back without a brand-new one. Arnold Jones never returned. His parents, like many before them, were defeated by the price of the school uniform.

Lucy was not paying any attention to what Mrs Sparks was saying. Instead she was looking hard at her hands. There was no sign of green anywhere. She did bite her nails but that didn't make them green.

Grown-ups, thought Lucy, do say the silliest things.

'Mindy Moxon,' said Mrs Sparks sharply, 'what are you whispering about to Tom Cole?'

'Nothing,' said Mindy.

'I don't like being lied to,' said Mrs Sparks. 'Give me that piece of paper you have just shoved up your sleeve.'

Lucy was now wide awake.

Mindy handed over the cutting about Blossom B.

'Ah!' said Mrs Sparks, smiling in a knowing kind of way. 'This time, Mindy Moxon, I am not cross.'

That surprised everyone.

Mrs Sparks went on, all sweetness and light. 'I see all of you are taking an interest in the wedding of the year.' She gave a little laugh. 'So am I. It is something that is very close to my heart.'

No one spoke.

'Well?' said Mrs Sparks, slightly put out. 'Is no one going to ask me why?'

'Why, Mrs Sparks?' droned all the children together.

'Because Mr Sparks, as you all know, owns Maldon-in-the-Marsh's premier garden centre, famous for its busy Lizzies, its gladioli and its dahlias. I think I am not letting the cat out of the bag if I say my husband, Mr Sparks, is bound to be supplying the flowers for the wedding.'

Here she beamed her red lipstick smile.

'Won't it be some big firm from London, miss?' Tom dared to ask.

There was complete silence. No one ever, not even Mr Sparks, questioned a word Mrs Sparks said. It wasn't worth it.

'No,' snapped Mrs Sparks. 'I have it on very good authority that Blossom B wants to support the local community.' She coughed and changed the subject. 'Now, I hope that all Miss Robinson's class have noticed our wonderful sunflowers.'

Lucy turned to look at ten proper earthenware pots each with a good shoot sticking out, though none as tall as hers. Without thinking she stuck up her hand.

'Mine is bigger,' she said.

The minute the words were out she wished they could be put back in her mouth again like bubblegum.

'Lucy Willow,' said Mrs Sparks crossly, 'it is not nice when girls tell boastful and silly lies.'

6
Best Friends

It took about a week for the carriages to be fully up and running, with electricity and plumbing and water. When it was all sorted out, Mum said Lucy could ask Tom and Mindy back for tea.

For Lucy it was a red-letter day, which means that it was very special indeed. It was the first time she had ever had friends over.

'Can we play with Ernest?' asked Mindy as the three of them walked back from school. 'We could

make him a race track and see how long it takes him to get to the finishing line.'

'OK,' said Lucy.

'Is it odd not to be moving?' Mindy went on.

'I sort of miss the clickety clack,' said Lucy. 'But I like being in one place. And having you two come home with me is great. Tom, you're really quiet. Is everything all right?'

'Sort of,' said Tom. 'I've just got a lot on my mind.'

They went round the bend and there in front of them were the three carriages that made up Lucy's home, looking very pretty sitting in the sunshine. A picnic table had been set for tea and on it was a large plate of sticky buns, Lucy's favourite thing in the entire world.

Mum was all smiles. She was

sitting with Stench in her arms.
For once Stench wasn't
screaming but gurgling merrily
away to himself, sucking his
toes.

'Oh, he's so sweet,' said Mindy. 'Can I hold
him, Mrs Willow?'

Just then Dad came down the steps carrying
a tray.

'Hello, kids,' he said. 'We're having a bit of a
celebration. I've got myself a new job.'

'Oh dear,' said Lucy. 'I like you being at
home, for pity's sake.'

'Well,' said Dad, lifting her into the air,
which was a bit embarrassing as there were
friends watching. 'It's only a part-time job. It's
working at a garden centre.'

'But Dad,' said Lucy, 'you don't know
anything about plants.'

'No,' said Mum, 'but thank goodness it isn't
that kind of job. All he has to do is work out the
accounts. There is no gardening involved.'

'It's not a job at Sparks's Garden Centre, is
it?' asked Lucy nervously. She didn't like the

idea of Dad working for the headmistress's husband.

'No,' said Dad, 'it's at Peppercorn Plants.'

'That's the one near our house,' said Tom.

'But I thought Mrs Sparks said that her husband owned the only garden centre for miles around,' said Lucy.

'No,' said Mindy, 'she said premier, whatever that means.'

'It means the most important,' said Dad. 'Well, Peppercorn's hardly counts. It's only a tiny outfit. The bookkeeper retired and Bert who owns it has only one ancient old walnut of a man helping, a Mr Mudd. The business is in a terrible muddle. I don't think this job will last for long, but it's better than nothing.'

'Mrs Sparks is a show-off,' said Mindy.

'That's not a very nice way to talk about your head teacher,' said Lucy's mum.

'Honestly, Mrs Willow, you don't know her. She's always going on about her husband and her horrible son.'

'She's certainly keen on extras,' said Dad. 'One minute we've got to send in money for the school Music Fund, the next we've got to contribute towards a Pet Guinea Pig Club. But let's forget about school. Tuck in. Help yourselves to what you fancy.'

After tea Lucy showed Tom and Mindy around. She told them that she thought the carriages must have belonged to someone really important, a long long time ago, just after the Stone Age.

'I guess so,' said Tom, staring in at the huge bathtub with its dragon's feet.

'Now that's what I call a swimming pool disguised as a bath,' said Mindy with feeling.

'It is,' said Lucy. 'I practise my swimming

strokes in it nearly every night, which is pretty handy I can tell you.'

'Well wicked,' said Tom.

Lucy collected Ernest from her bedroom and they took him out on to the grass. He wasn't too keen on racing so the three friends searched for tender shoots for him to eat instead. When he had curled back into his shell, they went down to the stream.

'Why were you sent out of class today, Tom?' asked Lucy.

'I don't really know,' said Tom. 'Something odd happened, and I can't work it out.'

'What is it?' said Lucy and Mindy together.

'Did you hear about Pam Potts?' asked Tom.

'The girl with the silliest name in the whole school, for pity's sake,' said Lucy.

'Yep, I guess,' said Tom. 'Anyway, she's now in Mrs Sparks's class.'

'What about it?' asked Lucy.

'Well,' said Tom, 'I was going to get some chalk from the supply cupboard for Miss

Robinson, and I had just opened the door when Mrs Sparks grabbed me from behind. She told me I shouldn't be sticking my nose where it's not wanted. Then she took the key off me, saying that only she was allowed to go into the supply cupboard. I told her Miss Robinson had given me permission, but she grabbed me by my collar and made me stand outside her office for a punishment.'

'You'd done nothing wrong, for pity's sake,' said Lucy.

'I know that,' said Tom. 'The thing is, I could see and hear every word of what was going on inside the office. Mr and Mrs Potts were there asking if Pam could go into the head teacher's class. Mrs Sparks said she would take some winning over, and cash would help. Mr Potts said would four thousand be all right, and Mrs Sparks said it would go towards the school swimming pool fund. I tell you, that's how Pam Potts got into that class.'

'So what?' said Lucy.

'That's not the strangest part,' said Tom. 'The strangest part is what was in the supply cupboard.'

'What?' asked Mindy and Lucy together.

'Bling-bling. More bling-bling than you've ever seen. All brand-new and shimmery, like Harrods' window at Christmas.'

'Wow,' said the two girls together.

'There wasn't one piece of chalk in sight,' said Tom. 'The school supplies were gone.'

'That's terrible,' said Mindy.

'What's it all doing there?' asked Lucy.

'Search me,' said Tom. 'It makes no sense.'

'Maybe we should report it,' said Mindy, 'but I'm afraid I don't think any parent or teacher would believe us.'

'Grown-ups,' said Lucy with a heartfelt sigh, 'are one of life's big mysteries.'

7

As if by Magic

The next day Lucy's sunflower needed
re-potting again, having sprouted up by a foot.
Miss Robinson stood and stared at it.

'Wow,' said her class. 'How amazing.'

'Alarming is what I'd call it,' said Miss
Robinson, sounding rather flustered. She took

off her glasses and
gave them a good
polish before
putting them back
on, just to make
sure she wasn't
seeing things.

'That's my
sunflower,' said Lucy
with pride.

'So it is,' said Miss
Robinson. 'Have you

noticed anything about all the other sunflowers that we planted at the same time?'

Lucy stared at the plastic cups and wondered if it was a trick question.

'There's nothing in them,' she said.

'Quite,' said Miss Robinson. 'It is one thing for a plant to grow a little bit better than anyone else's. It's another thing altogether for a plant to grow like this. In fact, it's not possible.'

She looked hard at Lucy.

'Do you know how this has happened?'

What Lucy knew was that adults liked things to add up. Like two and two is four and no other answer will do. Lucy could see by the look on Miss Robinson's face that things weren't adding up. 'Magic?' she suggested helpfully. 'Or Ernest, my snail?'

'No,' said Miss Robinson flatly. 'That's not possible, not even in Maldon-in-the-Marsh. I don't understand it.'

'What *did* you do to yours?' asked Mindy, looking gloomily at the earth in her plastic cup. It had nothing showing, not even the smallest shoot.

'I don't know,' said Lucy.

'Well,' said Tom, handing her his cup, 'could you do something for mine as well?'

'And this one,' said Mindy, handing over hers.

Lucy poked the earth with her fingers and again felt that odd tingling feeling. She pulled them quickly out of the pot.

'Well, maybe with your green fingers,' said Mindy, 'our class might have a chance to win the competition after all.'

If the truth were told, Miss Robinson felt more than slightly worried by Lucy Willow's remarkable sunflower. She was terrified of what Mrs Sparks would say when she saw it. In fact the very thought sent a shiver down her spine. Why, it was only yesterday that there had been that nasty scene concerning Tom Cole and a packet of chalk and the supply cupboard. Mrs Sparks had summoned Miss Robinson to her office and given her a piece of her mind.

'I thought I had made it quite clear that no one, and I mean no one, was to have the key to the supply cupboard,' said Mrs Sparks. If looks could kill, Miss Robinson would be dead.

'Mrs Sparks, we are low on some essential school equipment like pencils and exercise books and chalk.'

'Oh really?' said Mrs Sparks. 'And where is the money for these little luxuries supposed to come from?'

'They are not luxuries. They are essential to the children's education,' replied Miss Robinson, feeling herself to be in a lion's cage.

'In that case, the little dears had better start bringing them into school, hadn't they? Write a note straight away to the parents saying that you expect each child to be properly equipped.'

'It's the school that's supposed to supply these basic things,' said Miss Robinson. 'My

class are still waiting for their coursework on the Tudors.'

The phone interrupted what Miss Robinson was saying. Mrs Sparks hissed down the line, 'It's all safe and sound, tonight's good.' She put down the phone and looked at Miss Robinson. 'Where was I?'

'The Tudors,' repeated Miss Robinson.

'Never heard of them,' said Mrs Sparks. 'Do they live in the village? I haven't seen them about.'

'No, you know, Henry VIII, Elizabeth I,' said Miss Robinson.

'No,' said Mrs Sparks, 'you've lost me there.'

'Henry VIII,' Miss Robinson went on, hoping to jolt the head teacher's memory. 'He married six times and chopped off the heads of two of his wives — '

'And you think,' interrupted Mrs Sparks, looking shocked, 'that this is something that we should be teaching our children? A man who is beastly to his wives and gets away with murder? I refuse to have such a subject taught in my school.'

'He was a king and the head of the Church of England,' said Miss Robinson feebly.

'I know that, I am not stupid,' said Mrs Sparks. 'I have had enough of your mumbling and bumbling and your lack of organisation. I suggest that you buy these things yourself instead of coming whining to me every time you need a piece of chalk. Now get out of here.'

Miss Robinson had gone home that evening feeling very shaken and not certain what to think. How could Mrs Sparks not have known who the Tudors were? She was supposed to have a First in History from Oxford, no less.

As the evening went on a thought kept buzzing in Miss Robinson's head. Why was there no school equipment, and what had become of the school funds?

The residents of Maldon-in-the-Marsh were far too wrapped up in the forthcoming marriage of their local hero, Silverboots McCoy, and London's sweetheart, Blossom B, to notice anything else. Nobody was taking any interest in what was happening at the school.

As Silverboots McCoy would have said, they had taken their eye off the ball. For if they had been listening and watching, as was their usual way, they would have seen a dirty red transit van regularly pull up in the middle of the night round the back of the school and load and unload its wares. But, as I said, the wedding was the only thing anyone could talk about in Maldon-in-the-Marsh.

8

The Meaning of Green Fingers

Mrs Betty Peppercorn was a no-nonsense
woman. You didn't have to be a rocket scientist
to work out who wore the gumboots in the
Peppercorn household.

'I'm glad you're here,' she said to Dad when
he arrived on the first day of work. 'Bert's got
himself into a right old pickle and no mistake.'
She took him through a neat and tidy cottage
out into the garden, where at the back, hidden
by oak trees, stood a large shed. She unlocked
the door and with difficulty pushed it open.

Dad's heart sank when he saw the mess
inside. You could hardly get in for all the
papers and books lying around. The whole
place was piled high with filing cabinets stuffed
with letters, half of which had never been
opened. Receipts lay on the desk like dried-up
autumn leaves. Amongst them sat an ancient

typewriter, next to a half-empty, mouldy mug. What was inside had turned green. Seed packets were scattered in amongst the papers.

'I know it's a mess and no mistake. Bert kept this door locked and wouldn't let me see what a state things had got to.'

She went over and opened a dusty window, removed the mug from the desk, then brushed a dead fly off the typewriter.

'It took a while to get the key from him, I can tell you,' she said. 'He called this his worry den. Well, if it was me I would have been worried out of my skull by now.'

'Do you have a computer?' asked Dad.

'You must be joking,' laughed Mrs Peppercorn. 'Nothing that helpful, I'm afraid.'

'Oh,' said Dad. 'What did your old bookkeeper use?'

'He wasn't a proper bookkeeper. He was a jumped-up turtle of a man,' said Mrs Peppercorn. 'He couldn't be doing with

57

computers. Wrote everything down by hand.'

She took out a leather-bound book. The writing in it was almost impossible to read.

'Sure it's in English?' asked Dad, looking puzzled.

'I'm afraid so,' said Mrs Peppercorn. 'Are you going to tell me you don't want the job after all? You won't be the first if you do.'

'No,' said Dad. 'I'm very pleased to be working. It's a challenge, that's what it is.'

'You can say that again. When I saw the state of things I made Bert put an advert in the paper. You were the third person to apply. The other two took one look in here and we never saw hide nor hair of them again.'

'I'd better make a start then,' said Dad.

'That's the ticket,' said Mrs Peppercorn, and she left him to it.

By eleven o'clock Dad was in a complete muddle.

Mrs Peppercorn came back with a mug of coffee and a

plate of ginger snaps. 'How's it going?' she asked.

Dad looked up. His face said it all. 'To tell you the truth, Mrs Peppercorn –'

'Call me Betty, love,' she said. 'Everyone else does.'

'Well, Betty,' said Dad, 'I'm baffled. A lot of these papers relate to Sparks's Garden Centre, but you don't own Sparks's.'

'We did,' said Betty. 'It used to belong to Bert's father. One of the finest rose-growers of his day.'

'Pip Peppercorn, I take it,' said Dad.

'That's right, love,' said Betty.

'He sold it to Mr Sparks, then,' said Dad.

'Sold it, no,' said Betty. 'It was

more like daylight robbery. But that's all in the past. No good mulling it over. Though if by any chance you come across the last will and testament of Pip Peppercorn, don't hesitate to hand it over.'

Dad felt none the wiser, and was about to ask more when Betty said, 'Bert's rather lost heart for the business since his old dad died.' Her sunny face clouded over and she changed the subject.

'Do you know what Bert needs?' she asked Dad.

'More plants,' suggested Dad helpfully.

'Yes, that too. No, what Bert needs is a holiday, without a blooming flower in sight. Maybe he would get his old pizzazz back then,' she sighed.

'Who's Miss Fortwell?' asked Dad, looking at a dusty pile of papers.

'Now there's a grand lady. She used to supply us with plants, and still does when the wind's blowing in the right direction,' said Betty.

'At least that's cleared up these receipts,' said Dad.

'Do your best, George, that's all anyone can do,' said Betty, closing the office door.

By the time Friday had swung into action, Dad had a better grasp of the problems he was facing. Far from being an easy-peasy job it was turning into a Mount Everest of paperwork.

Dad was just about to set off on his bike for home that evening when Bert popped his head out from a greenhouse. Dad had hardly seen him all week.

'How are you getting on?' asked Bert.

'Getting the hang of it,' said Dad.

'I'm afraid we're understocked and a bit run down,' said Bert rather sheepishly.

'It's all right,' said Dad cheerfully. 'I'm getting on top of things.'

'Betty says you're a wonder. Look, why don't you bring your family over for tea on Sunday?'

'That would be lovely,' said Dad. 'Thanks.'

'Grand, see you then.'

'If Stench is coming, then why can't I take my snail?' said Lucy for the third time as they were getting ready to walk over to the Peppercorns' for tea. Stench as usual was screaming. Ernest as usual was quiet in his shoebox.

'Of course Zac is coming and no, Ernest is staying here,' said Dad firmly. 'I want us to make a good impression.'

'Well, that's not going to happen, not with Stench screaming, for pity's sake,' said Lucy.

Mum gave her a hug. 'Socks,' she said, 'you're going to have to get used to the idea of having a brother.'

'Never, never,' replied Lucy, crossing her arms and frowning. Lucy was good at frowning. 'I would rather have a snail than a brother any old day.'

Tea with the Peppercorns was much better than Lucy thought it was going to be. Bert said he wasn't too good at sitting still. And neither was Lucy.

'Would you like to come and see the plants?' Bert asked her.

'Yes, very much,' said Lucy politely as Stench started to scream. How much more of this screaming can a girl take? she thought, as she followed Bert out of the house.

As soon as she saw the plants in the greenhouse her fingers started to tingle. This was all most strange. She looked at her fingers. They were still pink, not a bit of green showing anywhere.

'Do you have green fingers?' asked Lucy.

'Of course,' said Bert. 'All gardeners have green fingers.'

'But they don't look green,' said Lucy. 'They're just rough and crinkly.'

Bert laughed out loud. 'Having green fingers doesn't mean that your fingers really are green. It just means you have a gift for growing things.'

'Is that all?' said Lucy, feeling even more puzzled and a bit disappointed.

Bert smiled. 'Do you know how tricky it is to grow things? Some people have no luck with plants while others can grow almost anything. Now, that's how you know a person with green fingers.'

Lucy thought about what Bert had said. Then she asked, 'Do your fingers tingle in a special green way when you're planting things?'

'No, they don't,' said Bert. 'Do yours?'

'Yes,' sighed Lucy and she told Bert about Ernest her snail and what had happened to the sunflower seeds and how surprised Miss Robinson had been by it all.

Bert listened very carefully. Then he said, 'Tell you what, shall we do a little experiment?' He picked up the nearest tray of seedlings. 'These,' he said, 'are sweet peas. Do you feel like putting your green fingers in the earth?'

Lucy did and her fingers tingled like anything.

'Did they tingle?' asked Bert.

Lucy nodded.

'That's good,' said Bert, and put the tray back.

'I don't think it will work,' said Lucy, 'because Ernest isn't with me.'

'Well,' said Bert, 'this is a good way of knowing whether it's you or Ernest that makes the flowers grow, or a bit of both.'

After the Willows had gone, Bert took a walk back down to the greenhouse. He wasn't sure if he was seeing things or whether it was because he had left his glasses up at the cottage, but those sweet peas did look bigger.

9

A Winning Ticket

It was shortly after Dad had started work at Peppercorn's that Betty scratched a lottery

ticket at the local petrol station and found, to her amazement, that she had won £25,000.

It was a shock from which she quickly recovered and she decided then and there that she was going to spend it on two things. One was a computer for the office. The second was a holiday.

Once Betty put her mind to something it would take trees to start walking before she changed it again. She came home with a deluxe cruise to Antarctica for two and a state-of-the-art computer.

Dad was as chuffed as could be with the computer. 'This will make the job much easier,' he said, carrying his prize down to the garden shed.

Bert, on the other hand, looked completely crestfallen when he heard what Betty had done.

'You won all that money and blew it on a holiday? We could spend it on getting a lawyer to look into our case!'

'No,' said Betty firmly. 'I am not throwing good money after bad, and that's an end to it. This has been going on for too long, Bert Peppercorn. We'll never know what happened between your old dad and Ricky Sparks. It will, I am afraid, forever remain a mystery which we have no way of solving. And the sooner you swallow that bone of contention the happier we all will be.'

'It's not losing Dad's business that bothers me,' said Bert, 'it's losing all that work on the rose when we were so nearly there.'

'This is just the reason that I'm taking you away on holiday,' said Betty. 'All this fretting is not good for your health.'

'And another thing,' said Bert, 'who'll look after things while we're away?'

'Everything will be fine,' said Betty. 'Mr Mudd will take care of the plants as he always has. George won't mind taking the orders and looking after the books. I'm sure he could do with some extra cash while we are away and if anything goes wrong, which it won't,' and here she said 'won't' very firmly, 'he can call on Miss Fortwell.'

'I suppose so,' said Bert, sounding unconvinced.

'It's not as if you have the contract for the wedding now, is it,' said Betty.

'In the past,' said Bert, sounding like a little grey cloud, 'we would have been the garden centre of choice.'

'I know, love,' said Betty kindly. 'Come here. Let's give you a hug.'

Dad thought it was a great idea for the Peppercorns to go away for a holiday, and

Betty was right: he was very pleased to have the extra money.

'Now don't you worry about a thing,' said Dad as he helped the Peppercorns into the taxi with their suitcases. 'What could go wrong?'

'Hold on a minute,' said Bert, 'there was something important I was going to tell you before I went.'

'Come on,' said Betty firmly. 'Just get in the car. I don't want us missing the flight.'

'Oh fiddlesticks,' said Bert, 'with all the packing and rushing around it's quite slipped my mind.'

'Well then,' said Betty, 'it can't be all that important.' And she closed the taxi door and waved goodbye.

Dad went back down to the office whistling to himself. He passed Mr Mudd coming out of the greenhouse, carrying a pot of spectacular sweet peas. Now, if Dad had known the first thing about gardening, he would have realised that that was no ordinary pot of sweet peas, for sweet peas don't grow that big. But then, what Dad knew about plants could be written on the back of a postage stamp.

It was a given in the village that Ricky Sparks would be supplying the flowers for the wedding. After all, he owned the largest garden centre for miles around.

'What's a given?' asked Lucy, leaning on her hands and listening to Dad talking to Mum. 'Is it like a turkey?'

'No,' said Dad. 'It means that it's taken for granted that Mr Sparks will do the wedding.'

'Oh,' said Lucy.

'You have to admire the Sparkses,' said Mum.

'Why?' asked Lucy. 'Mrs Sparks is terrible.'

Mum laughed. 'That's just because you don't like her. She does a lot of good in the village. Don't you think so, George? She's raising money for the new church bell and the school playground.'

'I suppose,' said Dad as he read out the flyer from Sparks's Garden Centre. 'Listen to this. *'Boa constrictors and other exotic snakes, Black Widow spiders, tarantulas, Venus Flytraps, goldfish and frogs for the pond.'*

'They seem to go in for a lot of other things besides plants,' said Mum.

Dad turned the flyer over. 'Look, here it says they do a good range of plants. Gladioli a speciality. Home-grown fresh-cut flowers for all occasions.'

'All I can say is thank heavens they are doing the wedding,' said Mum. 'Can you imagine the pressure you'd be under! I don't envy the Sparkses one little bit. They must be tearing their hair out by now.'

'At least,' said Dad, 'that's one thing that's

not going to happen in a million years of Sundays.'

Later, Lucy told Ernest that she thought Dad shouldn't have said that.

Ernest agreed it was a bit like tempting fate.

10

A Plant with Attitude

Ricky Sparks was a big man with small ideas. He had been into demolition until he met Petunia Peters at a karaoke night and the path of his life had changed forever. He had finally found what he was looking for: a thin lady with big ideas.

They had got married and had one son, a round boy called Lester. He was exactly the same age as Lucy, but unlike Lucy, Mindy and Tom, he went to Mullings School for Boys. The boys all wore blue blazers with brass buttons and the classes had desks that faced the black-board in neat rows. They drank milk and had buns in their break. Art was for sissies and the playground the size of a pocket-handkerchief. Games were taken in the park where Lester took great delight in bashing his classmates with conkers that he had soaked in resin.

In any other school Lester would have been called a bully. The teachers at Mullings School for Boys, however, thought he was a chip off the old block and that Britain needed more Lester Sparkses, not fewer.

It was Mrs Sparks who had persuaded Ricky to move out of London. They found all that their hearts desired in the sleepy village of Maldon-in- the-Marsh. It proved to be a perfect front for the Sparkses' other little enterprise – selling things that had fallen off the back of a lorry. In short, they dealt in stolen goods.

Getting hold of Pip Peppercorn's garden centre had been Mrs Sparks's idea. She had overheard a conversation in the butcher's, about Bert and Betty having to go up to Preston to visit Betty's mum. The butcher had

said that he didn't think it was a good idea
leaving old Pip in charge of the garden centre,
as the old boy was losing his marbles.

As Ricky said later, when the deal was done,
'It was like stealing candy from a baby.'

'I told you,' said Mrs Sparks. 'This is just the
beginning, my meatloaf.'

'Sound as a pound,' said Ricky Sparks.

It would be true to say that dainty plants and
Mr Sparks's very large hands were not exactly
a marriage made in heaven. His true loves
were his fish and the Venus
Flytraps.

'Now there's a plant
with attitude, son,' he
said to Lester. 'A real
man's plant, that is.'

Lester didn't like plants.
The whole of Sparks's Garden Centre could be
tarmaced over for all he cared. Snakes, though,
were different. One snake in particular was his
favourite, a boa constrictor called Sid.

'You ain't to sell him. You got that, Dad?' said
Lester.

75

'Sound as a pound, lad,' said his dad and so Sid continued to terrify customers,  shedding his skin and eating live mice.

'It's not nice, that snake,' said Mrs Sparks. 'I'm sure it's putting the customers off, Ricky.'

She was right. Blossom B had decided to pay a low-key visit to Sparks's Garden Centre without any of her entourage. She wanted to make sure the flowers were the right kind for her wedding. The first thing she had seen was Sid the snake in its dirty tank with half a dead mouse in its mouth. It was gross. It made her stomach turn.

'Hey, gorgeous,' shouted Ricky Sparks, coming out of his office. 'Want a personal guided tour?'

'No, ta,' said Blossom B, 'just having a look.'

'Come on, doll,' said Ricky, 'let me show you my Venus Flytraps.' He took her by the arm and walked her through the plastic curtains to where the plants were kept, with flies buzzing around overhead.

It was all too much for Blossom B. 'Get off me,' she screamed. 'Who do you think you blooming well are?'

'Ricky Sparks, entrepreneur and the owner of Sparks's Garden Centre.'

'Well, where's the proper flowers then?' asked Blossom B, brushing herself down to make sure no dead flies had fallen on her.

'Wouldn't you like to see the tarantulas first?' leered Ricky. 'They've got great hairy legs.'

'Oh just buzz off, you creep,' said Blossom B and she fled from Sparks's Garden Centre.

'Sissy,' called Mr Sparks as he watched her drive off in her Landrover.

'Do you know who that was, Dad?' said

Lester, sucking a lollipop and watching her speed away.

'No. A bit of fluff from your mum's slipper?' said Ricky Sparks.

'No, Dad, it was Blossom B, Silverboots McCoy's fiancée.'

'You don't say, lad,' said his dad, looking as if he had been hit on the head with a sledgehammer. For Ricky Sparks's next great love, even greater than the love he had for fish and Venus Flytraps and Mrs Sparks combined was, you guessed it, football.

'That's torn it,' said Ricky Sparks. 'Your mum's not going to be best pleased with me.'

The next morning at breakfast Mrs Sparks was reading the paper when she saw a large photograph of Blossom B under the headline *Wedding of the Year Brought Forward*. The article said that Silverboots McCoy had been chosen to captain the England team in the European Cup and so the happy couple had decided to marry earlier than expected.

'Well,' said Mrs Sparks, 'you're going to have your work cut out to get all the flowers ready.'

Ricky was very quiet. He had hardly touched his breakfast. He just sat there spooning sugar into his tea.

'You're feeling OK, I hope,' said Mrs Sparks, picking up the *Maldon Gazette*. 'You don't look yourself.'

Ricky snatched the paper from her. 'You don't want to read that, girl,' he said. 'You'll be late for school.'

Mrs Sparks could smell a rat. 'Give it to me,' she snapped.

Now Ricky may have been able to race a camel, jump through flames, even get rid of wasps' nests with his bare hands, yet when it came to Mrs Spark he had the courage of a wombat. Nervously he handed the paper back to her.

Mrs Sparks looked at the front page. There was another picture of Blossom B. This time the headline read: *Things aren't coming up roses for Sparks's Garden Centre.*

'What?' shouted Mrs Sparks as she read on. Blossom B was quoted as saying, 'I have a fear of snakes and spiders and I don't much like gladioli. So I will be looking elsewhere for my flowers.'

'Oh no,' shouted Mrs Sparks, sounding like a pan about to boil. Her face was so red that it looked as if steam might come out from her ears. 'You blockhead, you blabbering buffoon, you leered at her, didn't you?'

Mr Sparks cowered. 'It was a little misunderstanding. I thought she was just a bit of fluff, old girl. I was pulling her leg. I can't help it if she couldn't take a joke.'

Mrs Sparks rolled up the *Maldon Gazette* and started to whack her husband with it.

'You get that job back,' she screeched, 'or your life won't be worth living.'

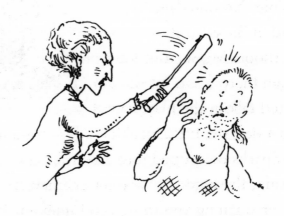

11
A Small and Terrifying Tornado

Ever since the news had got out that Sparks's Garden Centre would not be doing the wedding, a black cloud had followed Mrs Sparks around. A very black cloud indeed.

Each day her mood got worse. Everyone, especially Lucy, was keeping as quiet as possible. No one dared mention Blossom B or Silverboots McCoy out loud, though there was a lot of excited talk in the playground.

That day, the little black cloud surrounding Mrs Sparks developed into a terrifying tornado, the kind the weather channel are forever warning you to be careful about. For this kind of tornado can suck up and destroy anything in its path.

It happened just after lunch. Miss Robinson was teaching her class the history of the Roman Empire. She had just got to a really gripping bit about the Emperor Nero and the burning of Rome when the sound of giggling outside the classroom stopped her in her tracks.

'What's going on?' asked Miss Robinson, poking her head out of the door to see Mrs Sparks's entire class standing in the corridor.

'I don't know, miss. Kylie Kimble said the word wedding and we all got sent out of the room, miss. Jane needs the loo, miss.'

'Well, Jane, you'd better go. And Kylie, you go with her. Don't run, Jane, walk, that's a good girl. Oh dear,' said Miss Robinson, closing the door.

A moment later Mrs Sparks marched into the classroom.

'Miss Robinson, I am feeling most — ' She stopped in mid-sentence. 'What is that?' she asked, pointing past the blackboard to the windowsill where Lucy Willow's sunflower had shot up again, with Mindy and Tom's not all that far behind.

Mrs Sparks went over to the flowerpots and stopped in front of Lucy's. 'I might have guessed it,' she said. She stared fiercely at Lucy and then at Miss Robinson.

'Excuse me?' said Miss Robinson. 'I'm not sure that I understand.'

'Oh, you understand all right,' replied Mrs Sparks.

'Surely,' said Miss Robinson, her voice sounding shaky, 'you are not suggesting that I have been — ?'

'Cheating,' interrupted Mrs Sparks. 'You have let this child bring three plants that are nearly full-grown into school, all from her father's workplace no doubt. Do you take me for a complete fool?'

'No, Mrs Sparks,' said Miss Robinson.

Lucy bravely stood up and said, 'I have magic fingers. That's why they grew so fast.'

Mrs Sparks turned and roared, 'I don't like little girls who gild the lilies of their lies.'

'It's not a lily,' said Lucy. 'It's a sunflower.'

'Quiet, you snivelling brat.' And so saying she grabbed hold of Lucy's sunflower and hurled it to the ground. She did the same to Tom and Mindy's. Then, like a deranged moose, she stamped on the stems. 'This is what I do to cheats and whipper-snappers like you!' she said, glaring at Lucy.

'Mrs Sparks,' said Miss Robinson, close to tears, 'no one has cheated in this class. Lucy's plant has, I agree, grown remarkably well and it was all for the competition.'

'What competition? What are you wittering on about?' said Mrs Sparks.

'The one you told us that the governors were going to judge,' said Miss Robinson.

'Do you really think I would let them see this? It's an insult! Your class is disqualified from any competition,' shouted Mrs Sparks. She stormed out, slamming the door behind her and leaving a trail of earth and broken plants in her wake.

'Oh dear, oh dear,' said Miss Robinson, 'what has come over her?' And she knelt down to see if the sunflowers could be saved.

Lucy went to help while everyone else watched, all too stunned to say anything, fearful that Mrs Sparks would come marching back in again.

Lucy quietly picked up the broken stems with their heavy heads sadly bowed and asked if there were any bandages in the First Aid kit.

'I don't think there is much that can be done to save them, dear,' said Miss Robinson kindly.

'It's worth a try,' said Lucy.

Miss Robinson brought out the First Aid box and helped Lucy as she carefully re-potted each of the three plants, resting their broken stems on sticks and wrapping bandages around them. The sunflowers stood together looking like wounded soldiers returning from battle.

Lucy felt hurt and cross to see them so. The tingling in her fingers was very strong.

 She went round every one of the twenty-seven plastic cups and put her fingertips into them all before sitting down again.

'Mrs Sparks has gone too far this time,' said Miss Robinson, sweeping the rest of the earth into a pan. 'Too far.'

12

The Wrong Colour Scheme

One morning not long after these events the phone rang in Dad's office. It was Blossom B's personal assistant. Blossom B had heard that Peppercorn's supplied flowers, and wondered if she could come over and discuss the possibilities of their doing the flowers for the wedding.

Mr Willow's heart began beating so fast that he was sure it could be heard down the phone.

'Shall we say we will be there in an hour, Mr Willow?'

Dad stood stock still for a minute before he realised what had been said. Then he managed to stutter, 'Yes – good – look forward to it.'

As soon as he put the phone down he felt panic beginning to rise. He rushed outside to find Mr Mudd. 'They're coming,' 'Quick,' and 'Help' all seemed to come out of his mouth

together. Mr Mudd
stood and stared
bewildered at Mr
Willow.

'You feeling all
right?' he asked.

Dad finally
managed to explain.

'Oh deary me, oh
deary me,' said Mr
Mudd, plodding off
towards the greenhouse.

Dad threw his arms up in the
air and started to run about like a headless
chicken. Then to his alarm he saw Mr Mudd
set off on his bicycle.

'Where are you going?' shouted Dad. 'You
can't leave me, not now!'

'Got to get something. Back in a jiffy,' said
Mr Mudd.

'No you don't! Come back!' shouted Dad as
Mr Mudd slowly disappeared. His cry had no
effect, and he wondered if he would see Mr
Mudd again this side of teatime.

Half an hour later, to Dad's great relief, Mr Mudd cycled back with a trailer full of beautiful pots of sweet peas.

'Where did you get those?' asked Dad. 'They're blooming brilliant!'

'Well, there's a story,' said Mr Mudd. 'It's like this. Just before — '

'Not now,' said Dad. 'We haven't time. They'll be here in a minute.'

He grabbed a pot of sweet peas and put it in front of his office.

'The other thing,' said Mr Mudd, taking off his cap and scratching the top of his head, 'is quantity.'

'What?' said Dad. He was running backwards and forwards trying to make the best of the pots of sweet peas.

'I mean,' said Mr Mudd, 'we have quality, but we don't have the quantity, if you get my meaning.'

'And this is helpful?' said Dad.

'It's the truth, and whether it's helpful I couldn't rightly say,' said Mr Mudd.

'Look,' said Dad through gritted teeth, 'we

need to get a move on.'

'That's the other thing,' said Mr Mudd. 'Flowers don't understand things like get a move on.'

Dad had given up listening.

'Flowers will bloom in their own sweet time, and that's the nub of it,' said Mr Mudd. 'We don't have time.'

'We'll talk about it later,' said Dad.

Later seemed to come all too soon as a Landrover with darkened windows pulled up outside the front office, followed by several other cars and vans. Dad gulped. It looked as if the circus had arrived in town. Out got Blossom B, a man called Conrad who said he was the wedding planner, a bodyguard, a personal assistant, a photographer and a film crew from Murk's Music Channel. This time Blossom B was taking no chances.

'Hope you don't mind,' she said, taking a piece of chewing gum out of her mouth and handing it to her personal assistant. 'I'm having the whole thing filmed. It's going out in a special called *The Wedding Diaries*.'

Another car pulled up and a man with a shiny bald head and a briefcase got out.

'Oh,' said Blossom, 'this is Mr Gosh from Jolly's Chocolates. He's going to be paying for the whole thing. Isn't that right, Mr Gosh?'

'Ha, ha! Well, not exactly. Jolly's Chocolates are paying for half the costs and no more,' said Mr Gosh, his bald head going red at the top like a traffic light. 'In return, the wedding theme will be scarlet and gold, just like the

Jolly's Chocs scarlet and gold wrapper.'

'But I don't like scarlet and gold,' said Blossom B. 'I'm not having scarlet and gold. I want it to be pink and white. It's my wedding, ain't it?'

Dad left them to it and went back to his office. He had other things on his mind than who paid for what. His worry was the flowers. How was he going to get through this?

'I should say something,' said Dad under his breath. 'I should tell Blossom B that it's too big a job, that I'm an accountant, not a gardener. I should but I can't.'

'Everything all right, is it?' said Blossom B.

Dad spun round as she and the film crew crowded into his small office. 'Oh, don't worry. I know what it's like to be camera shy,' she smiled. 'Believe me, love, you get used to it. Just pretend they ain't there.'

This was a little tricky as Dad's office was now so crowded that it was hard to breathe.

'Shall we go and look at the flowers?' said Dad, anxious to be outside.

Mr Gosh came running up to Blossom B,

clutching his briefcase and his mobile phone.
He was mopping his bald head with a hanky.

'The d-d-design department — ' he
stammered.

Blossom B finished what he was about to say.
'The design department are doing pink and
white wrappers, right?'

'Yes,' said Mr Gosh.

'As my Silverbootie would say, a goal!'

Dad showed them round the greenhouses,
keeping his fingers crossed that no one asked
him any of the names of the plants.

'Wonderful old
roses,' said Conrad.
'You must be a genius
with plants.'

Blossom B sniffed
them with her pretty
little nose. 'Ain't that
something.'

'I lurve,' said Conrad, 'Flotsamera
Perfectimus Moore.'

Dad looked worried.

'Conrad,' said Blossom B, 'it's no good using

all them fancy words with twirls on them. They mean nuffink to me and by the look of it, Willow boy here ain't impressed either.'

Dad blushed as Blossom B took his arm.

'I like you,' she said. 'You talk straight. No pussywillowing about. You ain't rude, like that other codger with the ponytail. I'd like you to do the flowers. Think you can manage it?'

Dad should have said no. It was the word he was going to say, except out came 'Yes.'

'Great,' said Blossom B. 'I want a blooming lot of flowers and I don't like yellow. They don't go with the colour scheme. Get my drift?'

Dad nodded.

'I want all the flowers I see and more.' She turned to Conrad. 'What's that word you said, Conrad? That word I liked.'

'Arbour,' said Conrad. 'A wire frame covered in roses where you and Silverboots McCoy can exchange your vows. Now, Mr Willow, here's a list of the roses we'd like. I see that you have most of them. Of course we need them all in flower.'

Dad stared at the list as if the Martians had sent a text. He hadn't a clue what all these roses looked like, and the quantity! There were so many.

Dad was feeling quite giddy as he watched Blossom B drive away.

That evening Dad came home completely exhausted, muttering 'This is a nightmare.'

'I think you may have bitten off more than you can chew,' said Mum.

'I know,' said Dad miserably. 'But they are willing to spend bunches and bunches of notes. This could be the making of Bert Peppercorn.'

'Sweetheart, it's simple,' said Mum. 'Phone Bert and tell him to come straight back. Jobs like this don't come his way every day.'

'Why, you're a wonder,' said Dad. 'Why didn't I think of that?' And off he rushed.

There is no sadder sound than the endless

ringing of a mobile phone and the dismal
words 'Try again later' when there is no later,
just an urgent now. It turned out that Bert
hadn't taken his mobile. He had been under
strict instructions from Betty to leave the
blinking thing at home, and now she and Mr
Peppercorn were somewhere in the Antarctic
looking at penguins.

'So,' said Dad, after getting no reply, 'what
now?'

'I thought,' said Lucy, 'I should just tell you,
if it would be of any help, that I have green
fingers.'

'That's nice,' said Dad, not paying attention.
'What are we going to do?'

'Oh, George, I don't know,' said Mum.

'Maybe,' said Lucy, 'I could help.'

'What are you talking about?' said Dad and
Mum together, looking sadly at Lucy.

She could say it again, but what would be the
point? People just don't listen to children.

'What are we going to do?' asked Mum. 'For
goodness sake, George, you know nothing
about plants.'

'Well, I have Mr Mudd and he knows a lot,' said Dad nervously.

'Mr Mudd,' said Mum, 'is about one hundred and two. All he can do is potter. I don't think he knows the meaning of the words fast and urgent.'

'He's all I've got,' said Dad. 'Hey, honey, let's try and look on the bright side.'

The next day, when Dad was in his office, Mr Mudd collapsed into an urn of lavender and was taken to hospital.

13
A Bully and No Mistake

Lucy knew that her dad was stressed but had no idea quite how much trouble he was in.

'All Blossom B wants to see on her wedding day is flowers and the famous,' said Conrad.

All that weekend Dad looked pale and anxious. Mr Mudd had to stay in hospital for the time being: there was something wrong with his heart. Dad couldn't even go and ask him any questions, as it might be too much for him.

He took to calling the travel company over and over again to see if Mr Peppercorn could be contacted. He was told that this was quite impossible. All communication had to be kept for emergencies.

'But this is an emergency,' said Dad urgently.

'No,' said the calm voice of reason at the other end of the line. 'Weddings and garden centre problems are not counted as international emergencies.'

'Please,' begged Dad. 'Just give him my message.' But the phone went dead.

'You will have to tell Blossom B that you can't do it. For goodness sake, George,' said Mum. 'You are an accountant, not a gardener. This is not your fault.'

'I feel I'd be letting Bert down,' said Dad. 'He gave me a job, and he's been so kind. What would we do if I wasn't working? How would we pay Buzz Logan?'

Dad had a point. The rent was due any day now. Mum had no answer to the question.

Dad might just have given in and done what Mum was suggesting if it hadn't been for Ricky Sparks and his son Lester.

Mr Sparks came ploughing his way over the grass in his Jag. Father and son both got out, slamming the doors loudly.

Mr Sparks was an odd-shaped man who walked tipped forwards as if in a permanent battle with gravity. His long grey hair was tied back into a ponytail and he wore a T-shirt

with 5 on it, which was Silverboots McCoy's number when he played for England. He towered above Dad.

'Listen 'ere, townie, you've no right to come barging into our village, taking work away from true country folk. You understand me?'

'I'm sorry,' said Dad. 'Do I know you?'

'That doesn't matter. The point is *I* know *you*. The name's Ricky Sparks. Ring any bells?'

'No,' said Dad.

'Then it should, mister. How about Sparks's Garden Centre?'

'Oh,' said Dad. His heart sank. Ricky Sparks looked as if he meant business.

'Oh indeed, me old cock sparrow. Now, let me tell you I don't take kindly to you stealing my business. I'm a man to be reckoned with. Why, I've ridden a motorbike through four panes of glass and survived to tell the tale.'

'Why would you want to do that?' said Dad. 'It sounds terrible.'

'Because,' said Ricky Sparks, getting closer and pushing Dad against the carriage door, 'I'm hard, I am. I was trying to break a world record. I had to be stitched together. Comprehendo?'

'What?' said Dad.

'Don't mess with me, me old cock sparrow,' said Ricky Sparks with a glint in his eye.

'No,' said Dad.

'OK. Let me spell it out. Tomorrow you tell Blossom B that this job is too big for your puny garden centre. Otherwise there'll be trouble. Got it?'

'Yes,' said Dad.

'Sound as a pound,' said Ricky Sparks.

While Ricky was dealing with Dad, Lester had gone round the back. There he found Lucy, who was cleaning out Ernest's shoebox and making him a bed of fresh leaves.

Lucy stood up when she saw Lester. 'Who are you?'

'I,' said Lester, 'am a chip off the old block.'

'A what?' said Lucy, screwing up her face.

'I am Ricky Sparks's son, get the picture? What's in there?' said Lester, pointing at the shoebox.

'My pet Ernest,' answered Lucy.

'What's that? You got a tarantula in there?' asked Lester.

'No,' said Lucy, 'it's a snail.'

'Oh what a baby, got a little itsy-bitsy snail, has she,' said Lester. 'Well, little girl, if you

want to keep your pet, just tell your dad to leave off the flowers. You get me?'

'Get out of here,' said Lucy.

Lester began to swing his conker. 'Are you listening, pigtail girl? Otherwise that pet of yours will be shell only.'

'Who do you think you are, fatso glotso? You have no right to tell me anything,' said Lucy defiantly.

'What did you call me?' said Lester. He was beginning to swing his conker over his head when his father's large hand caught it.

'They got the message, son. Let's get going.'

The two of them got back into the Jag and drove away, making sure that they went through the biggest puddle and splattering mud on Stench's clean nappies as they went.

'What are you going to do, Dad?' asked Lucy.

Dad picked her up and for the first time that weekend, he smiled.

'I may not know anything about plants but I know a couple of bullies when I see them. And no one is going to bully me or my family.'

Mum gave him a hug.

'Blossom B will have her flowers,' said Dad.

'How?' asked Mum.

'I don't know, but she will,' said Dad, 'and it will be Bert Peppercorn's name in the wedding programme and no one else's.'

'That's the spirit,' said Mum.

'How?' asked Lucy firmly.

14

Perhaps
the Tallest Sunflower Ever

That Monday morning at school was a day to remember. Lucy found Miss Robinson standing like a statue in the middle of the classroom, her mouth wide open. There in front of her was a giant display of sunflowers. The tallest had broken through the skylight, and shone down, its head a brilliant yellow like the sun.

'Wow!' said Mindy. 'That's yours, Lucy.'

It was an

awesome sight. Miss Robinson, as if snapping out of a trance, said in a shaky voice, 'It is one thing for a plant to grow a little bit bigger than expected. It's another thing altogether for plants to grow like this. In fact, it's unbelievable.'

She looked at Lucy. 'Do you have an explanation?'

'Magic and green fingers?' Lucy suggested hopefully.

'I am beginning to think you might be right,' said Miss Robinson.

'Crikey,' said Mindy. 'Think what would have happened if you had planted a bean.'

'I guess it would been like Jack and the Beanstalk,' said Tom.

'Oh dear, oh dear,' said Miss Robinson. 'I shudder to think what Mrs Sparks will say.'

The head teacher had seen the sunflowers as she had driven into the school courtyard, their heads sticking out and laughing at her. She charged into the classroom like a rhinoceros in a sweetshop.

'This,' she shouted, 'has gone far enough.' She grabbed Lucy by the ear.

'What are you doing?' said Miss Robinson, startled. 'You are hurting the child.'

'Badly, I hope,' said Mrs Sparks, dragging Lucy to stand outside her office door.

Lucy stood there miserably, rubbing her ear. The walls to Mrs Sparks's office were thin and Lucy could hear her on the phone. She couldn't quite make out what Mrs Sparks was saying, though at one point she thought she heard a distant voice say, 'Sound as a pound.'

Mrs Sparks charged into the corridor. 'I've called your parents to the school. You can stand there until they arrive.'

Half an hour later the Willows turned up with Stench in his buggy.

'I'm sorry,' said Lucy, who was near to tears, 'I didn't do anything.'

'Quiet, no one said you could talk,' said Mrs Sparks, grabbing her arm and marching them all to Miss Robinson's classroom. 'There!' she yelled, pointing at the overgrown flowers.

Dad couldn't help it. He laughed out loud. 'If only Vincent van Gogh could have seen these. Think of the painting he could have done!'

'I see that you find this amusing,' said Mrs Sparks frostily. 'I don't. I think you should be ashamed of yourselves for encouraging your daughter to cheat in this manner.'

'To what?' said Mum and Dad together.

'You heard me,' said Mrs Sparks. Lucy was reminded of a toad that she'd read about in a newspaper that swelled up and then exploded.

'What are you suggesting?' said Dad, shocked.

'That you broke into the classroom over the weekend and smuggled in these ridiculous plants. I suppose you want publicity for your wretched garden centre.'

'But we didn't,' said Dad. 'That's an absurd suggestion.'

'We should talk about this in my office,' said Mrs Sparks. 'Follow me.' She turned on her heel, followed by the Willow family.

'Sit down,' said Mrs Sparks. She closed the door of her office and stood barring it. 'I have something to tell you. I have decided to suspend Lucy for a week. She is not to return until after half-term.'

'But you can't do that,' said Dad. 'Lucy hasn't done anything wrong.'

'I most certainly can. And I would remind

you that Lucy is a very lucky child to be allowed to come to this school. You wouldn't want her to lose her place here, I am sure.'

It was true that Mr and Mrs Willow had nowhere else to send Lucy. They sat in the office while Mrs Sparks went on and on, but it was no good. Lucy was to be suspended.

It was only when Stench started screaming that they were allowed to go home.

'I'd better get back to the office,' said Dad, getting on his bicycle. 'I've so much to do.'

Mum and Lucy walked back home, with Stench sleeping in his buggy.

'What was all that about?' said Mum. 'Mrs Sparks seems to be deranged.'

'Honestly, Mum, I truly didn't do anything, apart from having a tingling feeling in my fingers,' said Lucy.

Mum stopped pushing the buggy and gave her a big hug and a kiss.

'I don't think anyone did anything wrong, though it is a bit of a mystery how those sunflowers got so large so quickly.'

'I keep telling you. It's my green fingers,' said Lucy.

'Of course,' said Mum, laughing, and Lucy knew she didn't believe her.

They had just got home and Mum had put on the kettle when the phone rang. It was Dad. Lucy could see that something was wrong for Mum went as white as a sheet.

'Are you all right?' asked Lucy as Mum sat down hard in her chair.

'Peppercorn Plants has been trashed and there is nothing left. Who would do such a thing?'

15
Trashed

It looked as if a mad rabbit had been let loose to crash into every plant in Bert Peppercorn's garden centre. There was no mystery as to who had done this. The tyre marks of Ricky Sparks's Jag were all over the ground.

'We should call the police,' said Mum.

'Too late,' said Dad. 'The damage is done.'

Mum picked up a broken rose. She had tears in her eyes. 'Do you think that's why Mrs Sparks kept us so long at school, so he could come here? How could he stoop so low?'

'Most probably,' said Dad. 'I am beginning to think that there is no right or wrong when it comes to flowers and weddings.'

Forty-five minutes later, a policeman on a motorbike turned up. It had been raining ever since Lucy and Mum had got there and all traces of Ricky Sparks's tyre marks had been washed away. The policeman looked not best pleased to be called out to look at an enormous mud pie.

'So what did you say has happened?' he asked.

'The garden centre has been trashed. If you had got here earlier,' said Dad, through gritted teeth, 'you would have seen the tyre marks.'

'I'm afraid we're very overstretched at the moment, Mr Willow,' said the policeman. 'You may be aware that the wedding of the century is taking place here in a few days time and we have stars arriving from all round the world. It is our job to protect them and make sure that all security is in place.'

'We're supposed to be supplying the flowers for the wedding,' said Dad, trying to contain his anger.

'Well, it doesn't look like that's going to be happening,' said the policeman helpfully.

'Aren't you even going to investigate it?' shouted Dad as the policeman started up his motorbike and roared off.

'There's always my green fingers,' said Lucy.

'What?' said Dad.

'About those sunflowers. I have green fingers and they tingle and then things grow.'

Mum and Dad looked at Lucy as if seeing her for the first time.

'You what?' said Dad.

Lucy put out her hands and wiggled her fingers.

'They may look pink and I may bite my nails but in spite of that, they are magic fingers.'

'I can't see what that's got to do with anything,' said Dad.

'The sunflowers!' said Lucy.

It was like talking to a brick wall. Really, what was it about adults, thought Lucy, that made them so slow?

'I think,' said Lucy, 'it might also have something to do with Ernest.'

Dad was about to say he doubted that a snail had much to do with it when an old Rover came splashing up the gravel drive. Out got a very sprightly lady.

'Hello, are you Mr Willow? You called me, remember? Miss Fortwell, at your service.'

16
Miss Fortwell

Miss Gertie Fortwell was a tall lady. Her white hair was cut in a very smart bob and she wore a long flowing dress under which was a stout pair of walking boots. Her speech was what Lucy called very upright English and she sounded as if she came from an old black and white movie, the kind Lucy liked watching on rainy Saturday afternoons, where everyone spoke very properly and said things like gosh and jolly hockey sticks.

'Been away in Devon for the past week, got back to

hear your message on the answerphone and came straight away. Lord love us, what has happened here?' asked Miss Fortwell, looking at the broken glass in the greenhouses and at the huge mudbath that once was Peppercorn Plants.

Dad explained about Blossom B and the wedding of the year and Ricky Sparks's visit.

'Obnoxious man,' said Miss Fortwell.

'Wow,' whispered Lucy to her mum. 'What does that mean?'

'It means most unpleasant,' said Miss Fortwell, who overheard her. 'But don't worry. Every problem has its solution.'

'I wish I could believe you,' said Dad, sounding unconvinced.

'No good standing here like lemons. Best if you come round to my house for a cup of good strong tea. Then you can have a look in my greenhouses.'

Dad tried to smile and said, 'Thank you.'

'Mustn't fall at the first fence, Mr Willow, it's not what winners do.'

They all piled into the old Rover and drove

to Miss Fortwell's. She lived in a very pretty old house that looked as if it might only have a small garden. As Dad stared out of the sitting room window while Miss Fortwell got the tea, he said rather gloomily to Mum, 'Can't see where she would keep the plants.'

'Heard that,' said Miss Fortwell, coming back with a handsome tea tray with home-made cakes and scones. 'Not supposed to see the blighters. The greenhouses are out of sight. See the box hedge at the end of the garden where the statue of Cupid is?'

'Yes,' said Dad.

'If plants are what you're after, look behind that cheeky chappie. It's a sight for sore eyes. But first let's have some tea.'

She handed round the tea in proper china cups with saucers, which Lucy was most impressed with.

'I don't understand,' said Dad. 'Why hasn't Bert been getting his plants from you?'

'Bert lost his sparkle after his dad died, or rather, he lost interest in growing things,' said Miss Fortwell. 'Best thing Betty could have done is take him on holiday.'

'It all sounds very mysterious,' said Dad.

'Did Bert or Betty tell you anything?' asked Miss Fortwell.

'Just that they used to own the garden centre that now belongs to Ricky Sparks,' said Dad.

'Well, that's just the tip of the iceberg,' said Miss Fortwell. 'The trouble is where to start.'

'At the beginning,' suggested Lucy.

'Why not?' said Miss Fortwell. 'Good a place as any. Bert and his father Pip Peppercorn were both brilliant gardeners. Old Pip Peppercorn was one of the foremost rose-growers. He was developing a rare and beautiful rose that was going to take the market by storm. He and Bert worked at it day and night. They lived and breathed roses.'

'What happened?' asked Dad.

'Poor old Pip started to get ill and lose his memory,' said Miss Fortwell. 'It slowly got worse, but not so bad that Bert and Betty couldn't leave him and go and see her mother who was sick up north. When they came back Pip said he wasn't feeling too good, and a week later he died in hospital.'

'Oh dear,' said Mum. 'How terribly sad.'

'As if that wasn't bad enough, Bert found out that he had made a will leaving the garden centre to the Sparkses.'

'What happened to the rose?' asked Dad.

'Good question,' said Miss Fortwell. 'Everything to do with it had vanished. Mr Sparks wouldn't let the Peppercorns into the garden centre even to pick up their personal belongings. It was a tragedy.'

'Did they try and stop it?' asked Dad.

'Yes, but it was no good, the old boy had signed all the documents and even given power of attorney to the Sparkses.'

'What does that mean?' asked Lucy.

'It means those crooks could do what they liked with all Pip's money and property. It's a document that no one should sign lightly. The court said it was all proper and above board.'

'Was it?' asked Mum.

'Bert was sure the will was a forgery and that it wasn't his dad's real will. No way of proving it,' said Miss Fortwell.

'Does Mr Sparks know that you used to supply Bert?' asked Dad.

'No, don't think so. Don't trust that woman an inch, she isn't interested in plants, just money. That's what moves her boat,' said Miss Fortwell.

'I'm sure it was Ricky Sparks who trashed the garden centre,' said Dad, beginning to feel better and less cross.

'Wouldn't doubt it,' said Miss Fortwell. 'Don't like him, don't like her. They're a couple of rotten apples. Wish I could prove it.

The whole village seems to think the sun shines out of them. Come on, let me show you the greenhouses.'

She took them down to the bottom of her garden and through the tall box hedge.

'Now, I've kept the seeds and plants going, hoping that one day Bert would spring back and show everyone what a wonderful gardener he truly is.'

Dad's heart soared when he saw what was in the greenhouses; row upon row of plants, all about to flower.

'It's wonderful,' said Dad, jumping up and down, 'it's marvellous,' and picking Lucy up he started to dance, singing, 'thank heaven for little girls.'

'Dad,' said Lucy, 'stop. It's really embarrassing.'

'Can't see them from the road,' said Miss Fortwell. 'Otherwise Ricky Sparks would be down here with a steamroller.'

'Do you have roses?' asked Dad.

'Plenty of roses at the back,' said Miss Fortwell. 'Now, the only problem is time.

They'll need another three weeks to be in their prime.'

Dad said very quietly, 'You're joking. We haven't got three weeks, just until Saturday.'

Miss Fortwell was about to say a word she hardly ever used – impossible – when Lucy spoke up.

'If you let me help you we can do it.'

17
Suited and Booted

Ricky Sparks was down in the dumps. The phone hadn't rung at the garden centre the whole afternoon. He had all his three mobiles charged up, the office phone in his hand, and the walkie-talkie

beside him. He was in charge of the control centre and the silence was deafening.

Mrs Sparks had rung on the hour, every hour, but that didn't count. By the afternoon, there was still no word.

'Blossom B must know by now that Peppercorn's haven't a plant to their name,' said Mrs Sparks. 'Do you think that idiotic bookkeeper went round to see her?'

The very thought made little beads of sweat break out on Ricky's face. Something had to be done. He called his son.

It was Mullings' half-term and Lester was at a loose end. Bored with pulling the wings off flies and catapulting paper bullets at passers-by, he wanted something to get his teeth into and Dad had just the job.

Lester didn't go to Mullings School for Boys for nothing. He had learned that time was money, money was time.

'Sure, Dad,' he said. 'How much are you going to pay me?'

So a deal was struck. That's what Ricky Sparks was good at. Deals.

Lester's job was a doddle. All he had to do was see who was coming in and who was going out of Silverboots McCoy's mansion. Spying was right up his street. He had a walkie-talkie and six bars of Jolly's Chocs to keep him going. Every time the gate opened, Lester would ring and say, 'This is Beaver

calling Dad. Do
you receive me?
Over and out.'
But there was
nothing much to
report.

Mrs Sparks
had a
Governors'
meeting but she
came down to the
garden centre as soon as
it was over to ask her husband
what he proposed to do.

'What more can I do, me old girl?' said
Ricky Sparks, looking like a mangy lion penned
up in a very small cage. 'Lester's down there
keeping an eye on things and I've been here
waiting and waiting for the phones to ring.'

'You're sure you finished off Bert
Peppercorn's plants?' said Mrs Sparks. 'I kept
the Willows in the school office long enough.'

'Look, me old girl, I told you, nothing was
left standing. Everything's gone. Demolition is

my second name, remember,' said Ricky Sparks.

'Then what on earth's happening? The wedding's just round the corner!' screeched Mrs Sparks. She started pacing up and down the office. 'You'll just have to go round and say that you've heard there's been a bit of a calamity and offer to do the flowers your-self. Say it would be best if you were given the order, otherwise . . .' She stopped. 'Well, maybe leave that bit out. Just make it clear that it would be a mistake to go elsewhere.'

'What, me?' said Ricky Sparks. 'You want me — '

'Yes, *you*, washed, cleaned, suited and booted. Go and tell them,' said Petunia Sparks firmly.

'What, *me?*' said Ricky Sparks again. 'But I ain't good with words. That's your department. And,' he added in a small voice, 'she ain't that keen on me, old girl, remember.'

Petunia Sparks looked sadly at her husband's large, sagging tummy falling out over his trousers. At his grey, long hair and his dirty string vest.

'On second thoughts,' she said, 'I'd better come with you.'

18

A Lovely Bunch of Flowers

Miss Fortwell, unlike other grown-ups, had no problem in the slightest in believing in Lucy's green fingers. She had seen this kind of magic once before in India, though to be honest she never in her wildest dreams expected to find it turning up in Maldon-in-the-Marsh.

Being an organised lady, she had a plan for which plants Lucy should work on first.

'Roses, that's it, let's get you started on these beautiful thorny creatures.'

As Lucy had been suspended from school, she spent the rest of the day happily going round all the rosebushes with Ernest by her side.

The next day, she got up extra early and rushed round to Miss Fortwell to see if all her hard work had paid off.

'Come on,' said Miss Fortwell. 'Shall we see

how your green fingers have done?'

'I don't think,' said Lucy, 'that Mum and Dad believe that I can really do anything. I heard Dad say he thought the sunflowers were just a freak of nature.'

'Poppycock,' said Miss Fortwell firmly. 'I believe completely in extraordinary things happening. No doubt about it.'

They were greeted by a wonderful sight. All the roses were blooming. Even the seedlings had doubled if not trebled in size.

'I think it must be because of Ernest, my snail,' said Lucy.

'Well, whatever it is, it is the best bit of magic I have seen for quite some time. Do you know, Lucy Willow, if you carry on like this we just might surprise everyone.'

Lucy had never enjoyed being off school more, and there was so much to learn about plants.

'I always talk to them,' said Miss Fortwell. 'People may think I'm nuts but I don't care. Plants are just like us. They have their likes and their dislikes. I can tell they are all very keen on you. Take the roses. They are very vain, did you know that? They like to think they are the queen of the flowers. Always give you a good sharp jab if you don't tell them how beautiful they are.'

Lucy went round the roses once more with Ernest, telling them all how lovely they were and how if they carried on like this they would outshine all the other flowers.

By teatime Lucy had had a good chat with nearly every rose, poppy, delphinium, lupin and peony and every other blooming flower.

'You know, Miss Fortwell,' said Lucy, 'flowers are very gossipy.'

After school Tom and Mindy cycled over to see Lucy at Miss Fortwell's and report on what was happening.

'We have no school now until after half-term,' said Tom. 'Isn't that the bees' knees?'

'Why?' asked Lucy.

'Because Mrs Sparks can't get rid of the sunflowers. Yesterday the *Maldon Gazette* arrived to take pictures and today they had grown even taller and there were photographers all round the school.'

'Mrs Sparks nearly blew a fuse when she saw them all,' said Mindy. 'She told them to clear off.'

'Did they?' said Lucy.

'No, of course not,' said Tom. 'Anyway, a man came down from Kew Gardens and said that he wanted to take one of the sunflowers back to London with him. He said he thought it might be the tallest sunflower in the world.'

'Did anyone ask who had planted them?' asked Lucy.

'Mrs Sparks told the reporters that it was her class,' said Mindy, laughing. 'As if those stuck-up twits could grow anything! Oh Lucy, you missed the best fun.'

Lucy took her two friends off to see the flowers in the greenhouse. Tom and Mindy stood there open-mouthed.

'Wow, Lucy, these look amazing. Are roses supposed to grow that big?' asked Mindy.

'However did you do it?' asked Tom.

'Well,' said Lucy, 'I'm pretty sure that it's partly me and partly Ernest.'

'What do you mean?' asked Mindy.

'Well, I think my magic fingers might have something to do with Ernest. Every time I've made anything grow, he's been by my side.'

The next day, when everything was coming on a treat and Dad was beginning to think they

might be out of trouble, the phone rang. It was Conrad, to say he had been over to Peppercorn Plants and seen that everything had been trashed. He was most terribly sorry.

'No, wait,' said Dad. 'Let me tell you, it's all in hand. The van will be with you on Friday as agreed.'

'I'm sorry,' said Conrad, 'Blossom B is cancelling her order. I know things in the flower world can get nasty. But it's their big day. We can't afford any hitches.'

It was with a heavy heart that Dad made his way over to see Miss Fortwell.

'You should see the blighters!' said Miss Fortwell. 'Why, Lucy Willow has a magic touch and no mistake. It's truly astounding. We have hundreds of perfect flowers. Give them a few more days and they'll put the Chelsea Flower Show to shame.'

'It's no good,' interrupted Dad. 'Blossom B has just cancelled her order.'

'Can't have done,' said Miss Fortwell. 'She mustn't. If only she could see what we have here!'

They went down to the greenhouses. Dad's eyes nearly popped out of his head when he saw the plants.

'What did I tell you?' said Miss Fortwell.

'And this is all Lucy's doing?' said Dad in a small voice of disbelief.

'Yes, remarkable child,' said Miss Fortwell.

Lucy ran up to him. 'What do you think?'

Dad picked her up and hugged her. Never had he felt so proud of his daughter and it stuck like a fishbone in his throat to say that Conrad had cancelled.

'Don't worry. I've got a great idea,' said Lucy. 'Let's take Blossom B a big bunch of these flowers and tell her we have thousands more like them just waiting for her.'

Miss Fortwell and Dad both thought this was a brilliant idea, but would Blossom B see them?

'We'll have them delivered,' said Dad. 'Say they are from Peppercorn Plants.'

'Splendid,' said Miss Fortwell. 'Stroke of genius.'

19

A Little Lie

So it was that a large and very
beautiful bouquet of
flowers, all pink and white
and smelling as sweet as
romance, was delivered
to the McCoy mansion
and left on a marble
table in the hall just
as Mr and Mrs Sparks
were waiting to be shown
in to see Blossom B.

Petunia Sparks hadn't got to where she was
today without keen eyesight and the ability to
read anything from a hundred paces. Seeing the
words Peppercorn Plants sent her into action
and before you could say watering can, she had
pulled her nail scissors from her handbag,
chopped off the label and slipped it into her

pocket. She was just in the nick of time, for the butler came and took the flowers through the door at the end of the hall.

After a while the butler reappeared and ushered them into the drawing room. By this time the flowers were in a large glass vase, looking spectacular.

'I ain't got a clue who sent them,' said Blossom B, sniffing a pink rose. 'There's no label.'

Petunia Sparks did one of her butter-wouldn't- melt-in-her-mouth looks and said, 'Why, we sent them as a token, to show you what we can grow.'

'These are your blooming flowers?' said Blossom B.

'Yup,' said Ricky Sparks, holding his breath in for fear of bursting out of his trousers.

'Really?' Blossom B asked again.

Mr and Mrs Sparks nodded like a couple of nodding dogs in a car window. Blossom B still wasn't sure. She had a strong feeling she was being told a porkie-pie. She felt sure that if Conrad had known that Sparks's Garden

Centre had flowers like these he would have used them, snake or no snake.

'I can see that you are lost for words,' said Mrs Sparks grandly. 'But I do assure you that you will find no finer florist for miles around. As you can see, my husband has a way with flowers.'

Blossom B had not only a very pretty nose but also a good one for sussing people out and she hadn't taken to Petunia Sparks. Yet she had a big problem. Her wedding was this coming weekend and here was exactly what she needed. She had told all the newspapers that she wanted to support the village. This would get her out of a pickle without having to go to London.

'I'll think about it,' said Blossom B. 'I'll let you know by the end of the day.'

'What is there to think about?' said Mrs Sparks, a little too sharply. Then, realizing that she might have overstepped the mark, she softened her voice to a sticky flypaper tone. 'Surely you would at least like to see our flowers before making your decision?'

The thought of the snakes sent a shiver down Blossom B's spine, but Mrs Sparks, not missing a beat, said, 'Shall we say this afternoon, around four?'

The minute the Sparkses were back in their car, Petunia Sparks got on the mobile. She called Inter-Rosa and ordered them to bring down all the flowers they had right away.

'Money,' said Mrs Sparks, 'is no problem.'

'But, old girl,' spluttered Ricky, 'they're in London. That's going to cost some readies. We don't want to go spending money we ain't got.'

Mrs Sparks narrowed her eyes, and speaking to her husband as if English was his third language she said, 'We're getting in the plants so that Blossom B will give us the job. We're going to spend money to make money.'

'I think we should leave it, girl. I have a lorry picking up the stuff from the school tonight, remember,' said Ricky.

'Well, you will have to cancel it. The press are all over the place,' said Mrs Sparks. 'It's that ruddy Willow girl and her sunflower. So you'd better tell Stan that it's off tonight.'

Ricky looked none too pleased. 'It ain't worth all this trouble, old girl. Let the wedding go. We've got bigger fish to fry.'

'I've just ordered the flowers, haven't I?' snapped Mrs Sparks. 'Think of the business we'll get from this!'

So it was that early that afternoon a large van with Inter-Rosa written on the side drove up to Sparks's Garden Centre, a sight that did not go unnoticed by Mr Mudd, whose hospital bed just happened to look out over it.

20
A Skirmish

Mr Mudd rang from the hospital to tell Miss Fortwell what he had seen.

Lucy was sitting in the kitchen having a glass of fresh lemonade with a biscuit, so she could hear quite clearly what was being said. The words Sparks's Garden Centre sent a flutter of butterflies through her tummy. That usually meant that something exciting was going to happen or something bad.

Lucy decided it was bad and she slipped out of the house, leaving a note on the table for Miss Fortwell. Then she set off to find Tom and Mindy, who were making their way over to see her.

'I'm so glad you're here,' said Lucy, out of breath. 'I think the Sparkses are up to something. I've got to get to Blossom B and tell her about our flowers. Will you come with me?'

'Wow, this is exciting,' said Tom.

'Do you think she'll see you?' asked Mindy.

'She's just got to,' said Lucy.

They didn't feel that certain of success when they came upon Lester Sparks standing at the electronic gates, waving his resin-soaked conker at them.

'What do you want?' said Lester.

'None of your business,' said Lucy.

'Wrong,' said Lester. 'I'm being paid to make it my business.'

'Come on, Lucy,' said Mindy. 'Maybe we should leave it.'

'No,' said Lucy. 'You have no right to stop me. It's a free country.'

'Wrong again. Not when I'm about, because what I say goes. Get my drift?'

Lucy pushed past him and went up to the gates.

'Oh look at you,' jeered Lester, grabbing Lucy's jacket. 'Who's a brave little girlie with a silly snail?' He spoke into his walkie-talkie. 'Control Room. Enemy captured. Over and out.'

'Sound as a pound. I'll be down in a jiffy,' came the reply.

'Over and out, Dad. That's what you've got to say,' shouted Lester. 'Over and out. How many times have I got to tell you? Are you thick or something?'

At that moment Lucy pulled herself free and rang the bell beside the gates.

'No, you don't,' shouted Lester, pulling back

144

his conker ready for attack.

Tom charged at Lester. They started fighting, and Tom forced Lester down.

'Stop it,' shouted Mindy and Lucy. 'Stop it, don't be silly!'

Lester managed to get to his feet. He grabbed Lucy and twisted her arm behind her back.

'If you come any closer, I'll bash her,' yelled Lester. Mindy rushed at him. He pushed her away and kicked her so that she fell down and started to cry. Tom was about to charge at Lester again when a car drove up to the gates and a door slammed. Then a very firm hand lifted Lester up by his collar and held Tom back.

'What are you playing at?' said a voice they hadn't heard before, and there was Silverboots McCoy.

Lester stood with his mouth open doing a good impression of a goldfish.

'It was them that started it, not me!' cried

Lester. 'I just wanted your autograph for my dad's birthday. Them there tried to stop me.'

'Is that true?' asked Silverboots McCoy.

'No,' chorused Lucy, Tom and Mindy.

'In my book you get a red card for hitting girls,' said Silverboots McCoy. 'It's wrong. It's what cowards do and there's no excuse. Give me that conker.'

Lester handed it over, keeping his walkie-talkie out of sight behind his back. Suddenly the voice of Ricky Sparks boomed out all too loud and all too clear.

'Just keep them pinned down, son. Use force if you have to but don't let them get to Silverboots' bit of fluff. Otherwise they'll let the cat out of the bag. Get me?'

There was a moment's pause, then a lot of crackling and a very red-faced Lester had to stand there while his dad said, 'Over and out! See, I remembered this time. Old Ricky Sparks ain't that thick!'

Silverboots McCoy said to Lester, 'Scram. I don't want to see you round here again. Do you understand me?'

Lester set off down the road, looking crushed. Silverboots went over to where Mindy was sitting on the ground, and to her everlasting delight she was picked up by the world's handsomest man and put into a silver Bentley.

'Well, what are you waiting for?' said Silverboots to 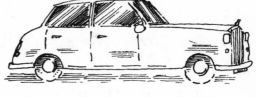 Lucy and Tom. 'Come on. Get in.'

They were driven up the drive and met by the housekeeper.

'This little girl has been in a scrape, Jodie,' said Silverboots. And Mindy was taken down to the huge kitchen where her knee was washed and a plaster stuck on.

'Better phone your parents to say where you

are,' said Blossom B kindly, coming out into the hall.

None of them had ever been in such a grand house. Why, it had clouds and cherubs painted on the drawing room ceiling and two sets of stairs, one at the front and one at the back.

'OK,' said Silverboots McCoy, as they tucked into a cream tea with cakes and ginger beer. 'What's going on?'

Lucy told Blossom B and Silverboots McCoy what had happened and how she and Miss Fortwell had managed to grow the most wonderful flowers to replace the Peppercorn stock.

'Who's Miss Fortwell?' asked Blossom B. So Lucy told them about her house and how there were all these greenhouses behind it.

'If only you would come and see for yourself,' pleaded Lucy.

'Look, I don't know a thing about plants,' said Blossom B, 'but I do know, sugar, they takes time to grow. Conrad told me Peppercorn's was well and truly trashed, not a plant in sight.'

'I know, but really, you should see them,' said Lucy.

'She's right,' said Tom, 'they're wicked.'

'Lucy's brilliant,' said Mindy. 'She grew these huge sunflowers that went through the roof at school.'

'I heard about that,' said Silverboots McCoy. 'It all sounded pretty unbelievable.'

Tom nudged Lucy. 'Go on, tell them.'

'No,' said Lucy. 'They won't believe me.'

'Tell us what?' asked Silverboots.

So Lucy told them all about her tingling

green fingers and about Ernest her snail.

'You don't believe me, do you?' said Lucy.

'No,' said Silverboots McCoy. 'There you've got me wrong. I believe you all right.'

'So do I,' said Blossom B. 'I wouldn't have got where I am today without a bit of the old magic.'

'One last thing,' asked Silverboots. 'Who do you think trashed Peppercorn Plants?'

'Ricky Sparks. His tyre marks were all over the place. The rain washed them away, though, so there's no proof,' said Lucy. She stopped talking, not sure if she should say more.

Silverboots McCoy started to walk up and down.

'What we need,' he said, looking at the three of them, 'what we need is a clever plan, to make it a level playing field. So that you can get your own back.'

'That's right,' said Mindy, 'but what?'

All of them sat there thinking.

'I've got it!' said Tom. 'I saw this programme

about Venus Flytraps on telly. Suppose Lucy were to . . . '

And he started to tell them his idea.

'That's it!' said Blossom B, interrupting. 'Tom, that would be blooming brilliant. What do you think, Bootie?'

Silverboots McCoy smiled. 'I think Ricky Sparks could do with a dose of his own medicine.'

21
Inter-Rosa

'It's not sound and we ain't going to make a pound. Not even a penny if we go on like this. Have you seen what Inter-Rosa charged for that delivery?' said Ricky Sparks to his wife. 'This is costing us a villa in Spain. I tell you, it ain't worth it, girl.'

'Shall I tell you what we are buying?' said Mrs Sparks, who felt she knew something about everything. 'We are buying us seats at the wedding of the century and we will be there milling with the famous. That is priceless.'

Now if the Sparkses had been paying any attention they would have noticed that their son Lester was unusually quiet and wondered why. However, they were far too wrapped up in making dreams come true to take any notice of him.

Lester didn't dare tell them what had

happened up by the gates of Silverboots
McCoy's mansion, or who had heard his dad on
the walkie-talkie. Or that he'd seen Tom,
Mindy and Lucy being driven up to the
mansion in Silverboots' vintage Bentley. He
had a feeling his mum wouldn't be too pleased
to hear this news.

'It's worth every penny,' said Mrs Sparks,
snatching the invoice away from her husband.
'Anyway,' she said under her breath, 'if we play
our cards right I'll be able to get a lot of this
back.'

Ricky put his arm round his wife. 'That's my
girl,' he said.

They were interrupted by the sound of a car
stopping outside the garden centre. Peering

through the grubby window they saw the object of all their hopes and dreams, Silverboots McCoy, getting out of his Bentley. He stood there, his black hair braided, with his perfect white teeth, his strong jaw and dark glasses making him look as if he had just left the set of an Action Man movie.

'We're in trouble, old girl,' said Ricky Sparks. 'I ain't got the labels off the pots. They still say Inter-Rosa.'

Mrs Sparks narrowed her eyes. 'You deal with the pots and I'll deal with the man.'

She quickly got out her make-up bag and powdered her nose. Putting on a plastic smile that would make a clown jealous, she went out to greet Silverboots McCoy.

'How lovely to see you again! And your fiancée. It will be a pleasure to show you round.'

'Blossom's going to stay in the car. She's not that keen on snakes,' said Silverboots McCoy.

'I am sure she will want to see the flowers,' said Mrs Sparks. 'All, I may say, hand-grown with love.'

'Nah,' said Blossom B. 'I'll stay put and Bootie can tell me what they're like, can't you?'

Before he could reply Mrs Sparks had taken his arm and quickly whisked him through to the reptile house where Sid, bored and dreaming of freedom, slithered in his sleep.

Blossom B sat in the silver Bentley watching her fiancé and Mrs Sparks go one way while Ricky Sparks and Lester sneaked off in the direction of the greenhouses.

'OK,' she said, reaching into the back of the car and lifting the blanket off Lucy. 'Remember, just the Venus Flytraps, nothing else.'

'I promise,' said Lucy, holding tight on to her shoebox with Ernest safely inside.

Blossom B got out of the car and opened the rear door, making sure the coast was clear.

'One more thing,' she whispered. 'If I whistle, you come back straight away. I don't want nothing bad to happen to you.'

Lucy made her way very carefully to the door of the reptile house. Sid looked up when he saw her and then sank down again. She could hear Mrs Sparks's voice getting nearer. Her heart thumped. Then she saw the plastic curtain and without another thought went through the flaps.

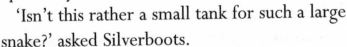

'This is where we keep our more exotic plants,' Lucy heard Mrs Sparks say.

'Isn't this rather a small tank for such a large snake?' asked Silverboots.

'Not at all,' said Mrs Sparks sharply. 'Cold-

blooded creatures like to feel cosy. As I was
saying, would you like to come and look at the
more exotic flowers?'

'No,' said Silverboots. 'Venus Flytraps aren't
Blossom's thing.'

And to Lucy's great relief, she saw them
walk away. There wasn't a moment to lose. But
– and here is one of those buts that you just
don't need when you have less than a minute
to do something important – her fingers
weren't tingling. She was too scared to feel
anything but fear. Oh come on, come on, said

Lucy under her breath. Ernest, we must do something. She looked around at the Venus Flytraps. They were such ugly plants, all prickly and snappy with flies buzzing around.

Mrs Sparks was talking outside. 'The trouble is that Mr Willow, who I believe you've met, is really an accountant, not a gardener. Between you and me, dear, I wouldn't be surprised if he wasn't the one who demolished Peppercorn Plants to get the insurance money.'

'Really,' said Silverboots.

'You do know that Bert Peppercorn, the owner of the garden centre, is away on holiday, don't you?' said Mrs Sparks. 'Now follow me and I'll show you our gladioli.'

Suddenly Lucy's fingers began to tingle as they had tingled before. With the speed of light she went round and touched the stem of every Venus Flytrap, once, twice and then a third time for good measure.

And then, making sure she wasn't seen, she ran back to the silver Bentley.

'Cor, you took your time,' said Blossom B, putting the blanket over her again.

A few minutes later, Lucy heard footsteps on the gravel.

'It's been a pleasure,' said Mr and Mrs Sparks together, seeing Silverboots McCoy into his car.

'I'm sure the flowers would have been right up your street,' said Ricky Sparks, grinning at Blossom B through the car window.

Mrs Sparks nudged her husband hard in the ribs so that he stood up straight.

'Such a pity you haven't met our son,' said Mrs Sparks. 'He's a number one fan of yours.'

Silverboots McCoy started the engine and pushed the button to open his window.

'I have already met your son, Lester,' he said. 'You should tell him from me not to go round hitting people, especially not girls. And by the way,' he added, 'if we'd wanted our flowers from Inter-Rosa we would have ordered them direct.'

Ricky Sparks began to turn yellow.

'I don't know what game you two are playing,' continued Silverboots, 'but I'm sure going to find out.'

22

Blooming Ada

Dad had gone over to Miss Fortwell's, to tell her that Lucy had called saying that she was up at Silverboots McCoy's mansion.

'One has to take one's hat off to that child. A fighter, that's what she is,' said Miss Fortwell, getting out the hose.

'Headstrong, more like,' laughed Dad. 'I don't know what good it will do. Anyway, she's having tea with them.'

'You should have a little more faith in that girl of yours, if you don't mind my saying so,' said Miss Fortwell.

Dad took the hose from her. 'Maybe you're right. I'll do this.'

'Thirsty little blighters,' said Miss Fortwell, and she left him to go up to the house.

Dad had been working away for about an hour when he heard wheels crunching on the

gravel. The next thing he knew, there were
Blossom B and Silverboots McCoy, with Lucy,
Tom and Mindy. Dad was so startled that he
dropped the hose. It
rose up like a snake
and squirted water at
him as he ran about
the greenhouse trying
to catch it.

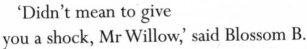

   Tom and Mindy
burst out laughing and
Lucy wondered if her
dad could be any more
embarrassing and silly.

   'Didn't mean to give
you a shock, Mr Willow,' said Blossom B.

   'You got our bouquet, then?' asked Dad as at
last he managed to turn the hose off and wipe
his face with his hankie.

   Blossom didn't reply. She was just gazing
wide-eyed at the roses.

   'Blooming Ada,' she said. 'Ain't these the
business! What do you think, Bootie?'

   The three friends left them to it and went off

to find Miss Fortwell.

'They're here,' said Lucy, rushing up to her.

'Well done, old thing,' said Miss Fortwell. 'I told your father to have a little more faith. I hope they're impressed.'

They returned to find that Silverboots and Blossom B were both standing there chatting away to Dad as if they had been friends forever.

Silverboots shook Miss Fortwell's hand.

'Lucy tells me that without you, Peppercorn's would be history.'

Miss Fortwell blushed. 'Well, not really. Without Lucy it might have been somewhat tricky. Now you're here, would you like to see the rest?'

'You mean there's more?' said Blossom B.

'Oh yes,' said Dad, 'lots more. Shall I lead the way?'

'I tell you,' said Blossom B, 'I don't think any posh London firm could beat them roses.'

'You've got the job back,' said Silverboots to Dad.

'We won't let you down,' said Dad, dancing a little jig and tripping over the hose again. This

time even Lucy found
it funny.

'How about a drink
before you leave?
Then we can work
out the order,' said
Miss Fortwell.

'Sounds good to
me,' said Silverboots
McCoy.

'Now tell me, Mr
Willow,' said Blossom
B, taking Dad's arm.
'Lucy says you live in a train. What's that like,
then?'

Lucy watched them go up to the house.

'It's going well,' said Mindy.

'About time, for pity's sake,' said Lucy with
feeling.

The next day Lucy was very surprised to find
that Miss Fortwell thought it would be better if
she didn't do anything at all to the plants.

'You mean Ernest and me aren't needed?' asked Lucy, who was quite prepared to keep working away. 'Are you sure?'

'Yes, for the time being,' said Miss Fortwell. 'Don't want the blighters to get too big. At the rate they're growing now everything should be perfect for the wedding.'

'So what does that mean?' asked Lucy.

'It means you can go and play,' said Dad, 'and if we need you and your magic fingers we'll come and find you.'

'Great,' said Lucy, punching the air with excitement. She felt pleased that her job was done. 'I'll be with Tom and Mindy down by the stream.'

'Be safe,' Dad called and he went back to the phone, to hire a van to take the first load of roses up to the mansion. Conrad had told him that he wanted to keep all the flowers for the church and the reception in the marquee. He felt it would be safer as the marquee had its very own state-of-the-art temperature control system, so that the flowers would be neither too hot nor too cold.

The next two days, while Dad, Mum and Miss Fortwell were working flat out, Lucy spent her time down by the stream. The weather being hot and the stream being cool, the three of them busied themselves paddling and splashing about. Lucy, who always took Ernest everywhere with her, had left the shoebox where it

was safe and dry in the hollow of a tree.

Everything, she thought, was bound to be all right now that Peppercorn's were doing the flowers for the wedding.

Little did she know that her troubles were just beginning.

23
Plans and Plants

Lester had been thinking things over. He had tried to tell his mum what he thought, but she wasn't in a listening kind of mood.

'Don't you Mum me,' Mrs Sparks snapped at her beloved son. 'You are one of the main reasons this has all gone pear-shaped.'

She was still fuming over the wedding and what was happening up at the school. Much to her fury, a man from *The Guinness Book of Records* had turned up to measure the sunflowers.

'I need this like a hole in the head,' she had shouted at Lester. 'I'd like to take an axe and chop them ruddy sunflowers down piece by little piece.'

Lester had a nasty feeling that if she was this upset about the sunflowers she would be even more horrified by what he had to say.

'I just thought you'd like to know,' started Lester, swinging his conker from side to side.

Mrs Sparks grabbed it from him. 'This is confiscated until further notice.'

'Mum,' cried Lester, 'that ain't fair.'

'Life ain't fair,' shouted his mother, flicking him hard on the cheek. Feeling fed up, Lester went off to find his dad. Maybe he'd be in a listening mood.

'Not now, son, I have bigger fish to fry,' said Ricky, taking no notice of Lester. Which was a pity, for if either of his parents had listened to what Lester had to say, things might well have turned out differently. For a start, Ricky Sparks would have known that his beloved Venus Flytraps were growing in a way that no Venus Flytraps had grown before. Lester had been watching them with interest and he was pretty sure Lucy Willow and her snail had something to do with it all.

Since neither of his parents was the slightest bit interested, Lester came up with a plan of his own.

Helping himself to a large multi-coloured lollipop, he went back down to the stream, where for the last couple of days he had been busy doing what he did best, spying. He knew just where Lucy had put the snail. He tiptoed over to the tree. Then, when the three friends had their backs to him, he quickly snatched the shoebox and put it inside his blazer.

He was just about to sneak away when a twig cracked loudly under his feet; so loudly that Tom spun round and, seeing Lester running away, shouted,

'Hey, come back!' But Lester made a quick sprint out of there, dropping his lollipop as he ran.

Back at the house, he took the shoebox up to his room and opened it.

I don't know what he was expecting, but he felt mighty disappointed to see an ordinary common garden snail with a boring brown shell. Ernest, you will be glad to hear, was sensibly curled up inside.

Lester took the snail down to where his dad kept the Venus Flytraps and let him go. He liked the idea of the Flytraps growing even bigger than they were already, and wondered what they might eat. Flies might not be enough. Maybe, like Sid, they'd like a mouse or a cat, even a dog, or – here Lester chuckled – even a human.

Ricky Sparks was spinning round and round on his chair, drumming his fingers on the desktop. He had been drinking Gorilla's Corolla. It was supposed to give you jungle strength. He was on his fourth can and looked as if he was ready to swing into action when Lester came into the office.

'I just thought I'd tell you — ' said Lester.

'They've no right to take that job away from me. And the money we've wasted on getting those ruddy flowers delivered from Inter-Rosa! I'll tell you this for nothing, son. It wasn't sound and it weren't worth a pound.'

Lester was relieved to see that he was no longer in the doghouse, but thought it best not to say anything about the Venus Flytraps.

'What are you going to do?' he asked.

'I've got to do some thinking,' said Ricky Sparks. 'And that ain't that easy. Do they teach you thinking at your school?'

'No,' said Lester, 'you have to do that out of school, in your own time.'

Just then the phone rang. Ricky picked it up.

'Stan, me old cock sparrow, how's tricks? Just a mo,' he said, turning to Lester. 'Go on, son, get out of here. Skedaddle.'

Lester stood outside the office door so that he could hear what was being said.

'Look, Stan, I told you not tonight, the school's crawling with the press.'

A few squeaks could be heard down the phone.

'Tell Fat Harry he'll have his stuff when all this has cooled down,' said Ricky.

Lester could hear someone shouting at the other end of the line.

'It's not my fault,' said Ricky. 'I tried to tell the old girl but she's got a bee in her bonnet about doing the flowers for Silverboots' wedding.'

More shouting.

'I know, Stan, I agree . . .' Then Ricky Sparks said, 'All right, tonight it is. Don't worry, old Ricky won't let you down, as sound as a pound.'

Miss Robinson too had been thinking things over. Sitting in her kitchen and stroking her rather large and overfed cat, she had said to herself, 'I just know something fishy is going on at school.'

Mackerel purred. He had just eaten a tin of the finest sardines known to pussycats.

'Why are there no pencils? Where are the art materials? What has happened to the school funds?' asked Miss Robinson. She got up and started to walk back and forth. 'And another thing,' she said, 'why did that woman get so cross with Tom Cole when he opened the supply cupboard?'

Mackerel had lost interest and gone out through the catflap, leaving Miss Robinson with a lot of unanswered questions.

'Oh dear, oh dear,' she said. 'And then all the fuss that Mrs Sparks made over the wedding. Not to mention the fact that she didn't know who the Tudors were. All most odd. There are so many things that just aren't right.'

By the afternoon Miss Robinson had come up with a plan.

'I need to get myself back into the school, half-term or no half-term. I need to find out once and for all what's happening.'

24

The Revenge of the Venus Flytrap

Venus Flytraps, when doubled, trebled or quadrupled in height, look like plants from Mars. And once they grow that big, flies no longer fill the empty gaps. Lester was right. Plants that size need something bigger to get their teeth into.

So it was that on the night before the wedding Mrs Sparks was woken about two in the morning by a strange noise. A sort of snapping and creaking sound.

Ricky Sparks had just got home from paying a little visit. He was sitting on the end of the bed dressed in a security guard's uniform, busily undoing his jacket and looking forward to being in dreamland.

'How did it go?' asked Mrs Sparks in a sleepy voice.

'Like clockwork, old girl. Your Ricky has thrown a spanner in the works and no mistake.'

'Good,' said Mrs Sparks. 'That will teach them. Go on, make us a cup of tea.' She stopped. 'Shut up. Listen, can you hear that?'

Ricky was now in his jimjams. 'Can't hear a ruddy thing, old girl.'

Mrs Sparks looked at her husband. He knew just what that look meant. 'Not now,' he said. 'I'm tired, old girl, and it's dark out there.'

'I am not going to ask you twice,' said Mrs Sparks, her eyes flashing.

Ricky grunted. 'Sound as a pound.' He put on his dressing-gown and made his way back downstairs.

Mrs Sparks went back to sleep, only to be woken by the mobile phone ringing. There was a muffled cry of 'Help!' There was no mistaking the voice, even muffled. It was that of her husband.

Mrs Sparks got out of bed, put on her Gucci slippers, wrapped her Prada dessing-gown around her, and went off in search of her husband. Not finding him in the kitchen, she went cursing and shouting out into the dark night, torch and mobile in hand, and made her way towards the garden centre, where she could hear cries of 'Help!' coming from behind the plastic curtains.

Something lunged towards her. Mrs Sparks let out a scream. It was an enormous Venus Flytrap. She could see her husband caught in the clutches of an even bigger plant. It looked like a creature from outer space.

'Do something, old girl!' shouted Ricky. 'Get help! It's got my ponytail!'

Mrs Sparks quickly shut the door and turned back towards the house. For once in her life she had no idea what to do. She flashed her torch, and froze.

Now if there was one thing that made Petunia Sparks's legs turn to jelly, it was the sight of a snail. And here were hundreds upon hundreds of snails.

'Help,' screamed Mrs Sparks. 'Help me.'

If any of the inhabitants of Maldon-in-the-Marsh had been awake at that time and had happened to be looking out of their window, they would have seen the strangest of sights: the head teacher of the village school running out of Sparks's Garden Centre and following a most odd path that led to the church. What they might not have seen were the snails that lined either side of the path.

Mrs Sparks, now quite beside herself with fear, ran to the church door, pushed it open and rushed in, slamming it shut behind her.

This was a nightmare. Mrs Sparks wished she hadn't dropped her mobile phone. She flashed her torch around the empty pews. To her horror a snail was looking straight at her in a knowing kind of way, its two eyes out on stalks. It was moving slowly towards her.

Mrs Sparks ran to where the bell ropes lay. She had forgotten that there was only an old broken bell up in the belfry. That was something she should have known, since the money from the funds for the new bell had bought her a villa in Spain.

No, Mrs Sparks
was not thinking
straight. She pulled
on the old bell rope,
remembering too
late as the rope
whisked round her
ankles and her
middle, shooting her
with the speed of a
rocket up into the
belfry with the bats.

Ernest watched
her go. Then he slowly made his way back out
through the crack in the church door to thank
his friends for their help.

25
Bling-Bling

It was a very busy night in Maldon-in-the-Marsh, and several of its residents had had no sleep whatsoever.

Miss Robinson had made her way back into the school, past her classroom with its enormous sunflowers, tiptoeing up the corridor towards the head teacher's office, her heart thumping, hoping against hope that the caretaker wouldn't wake up.

Carefully she opened the door to the office. Carefully she looked at the papers on Mrs Sparks's desk. The papers rustled, sounding to Miss Robinson like an alarm bell going off.

Thinking someone must have heard her she hid quickly under the desk. That was when she saw the little button. She waited a moment to make sure the coast was clear, then pushed it. Much to her surprise a secret drawer sprang

open. Not wishing to
waste another
moment, Miss
Robinson shone her
torch in on a pile of
documents.

The first words she
saw were 'The last
Will and Testament of
Philip Peppercorn.'

'Oh dear, oh dear,
whatever's that doing
here?' said Miss Robinson to herself. 'This
can't be right.'

Suddenly a beam of light shone in. Miss
Robinson hastily crawled into the outer office
and this time hid behind a filing cabinet.

There were footsteps coming up the
corridor. Then someone called in a gruff
whisper, 'That you, gaffer?'

Miss Robinson wondered if her heart could
beat any faster or louder as a man appeared,
wearing a balaclava. He shone his torch into
Mrs Sparks's office. Then he went over to the

supply cupboard and got a key out of his pocket.

'The cheek!' thought Miss Robinson as whoever it was turned the cupboard light on. There in front of her was a sight that nearly made her eyes pop out of her head. Jewellery. More bling-bling than she had ever seen. It was a treasure chest. It positively glittered.

Miss Robinson waited and watched. Then, when the man in the balaclava had filled up a sack and taken it out to a waiting van, Miss Robinson, with trembling fingers, called 999.

26

A Gruesome Sight

Lester was woken very early in the morning by the screaming of a siren and a blue light flashing through the curtains. He got out of bed and sloped down the stairs to see what the hullabaloo was about.

The sight that greeted his eyes was bewildering, to say the least. There were police cars, a fire engine and an ambulance. Men in white suits were walking about. The greenhouse that housed the Venus Flytraps was cordoned off with police tape, and he could see clearly that several panes of glass were broken. The plants had their heads half in and half out.

'Cor, then, that snail must have had something to do with it,' said Lester, yawning. 'What's going on?' he asked a policeman.

'There's been an incident,' said the policeman.

'What kind of incident?'

'Best if you stand back, lad,' said the policeman. 'It's a gruesome sight.'

Lester liked gruesome sights. Taking no notice, he went under the police tape and into the greenhouse. It was enough to give you the heebie jeebies.

'Wow,' said Lester, seeing his dad in the clutches of the scariest plant he had ever seen. It was like being on a film set.

'Get out of here, son,' shouted Ricky. 'It ain't safe.'

One of the smaller Venus Flytraps bent over and grabbed at Lester, catching his pyjama top.

'Step back, please,' said a man wearing a mask and a white spacesuit. He was holding a spray. He squirted something on the plant and Lester was free. Without being asked a second time he quickly found his way outside, still hopeful that he might be dreaming. Just then a man walked past him with Sid, his snake.

'Hey, where are you taking my snake?' shouted Lester.

'Your snake?' said the man. 'You should be

ashamed of yourself, keeping a snake this size
in a fish tank.'

'It grew,' said Lester.

'This,' said the man, 'is a very rare
Amazonian Malfortus Constricta.'

'Oh yeah,' said Lester, none the wiser. 'We
call him Sid.'

'It is a fruit-eating snake,' said the man. 'It's
suffering badly from hairballs in its insides
because of the wrong diet.'

'Really?' said Lester. 'We feed it mice.'

'The cruelty,' said the man, patting Sid on the head.

'Wow,' said Lester, looking impressed. 'I wouldn't do that. He's got poisonous fangs.'

'I've taken the precaution of milking its teeth,' said the man.

'Come again?' said Lester.

'I'm taking him to the reptile house in the London Zoo, where he belongs,' said the man, carefully putting Sid in his car. 'He'll be properly cared for there.'

'Wait,' said Lester desperately. The man took no notice and as he drove away, Lester thought he saw Sid smile.

'Where's your mother?' asked a policeman.

'That man,' said Lester, 'has just stolen my snake.'

'No he hasn't. Now, can you tell me where your mother is?' said the policeman.

'Don't know, don't care,' said Lester. 'I want Sid back.'

Just at that moment Ricky was brought out,

covered in gunge and dead flies. He was taken
to a waiting ambulance and wrapped in a
blanket and given a cup of hot sweet tea to
drink while they checked him over. Lester
went and sat beside him.

'Where's your mum?' asked Ricky.

'Funny, that's just what that policeman
asked,' said Lester.

'Your old dad and mum are in a spot of
bother, son,' said Ricky, looking round to make
sure no one was in hearing distance. 'In other
words, things ain't sound and we owe more
than a pound.'

'What do you mean?' asked Lester.

'It means we are in sticky toffee without a
sweet wrapper, if you get my meaning.'

Lester sighed. 'They've taken my snake, Dad.
A man drove away with him — '

'Listen, son, forget the snake. He's the least
of our troubles. We've got to get out of here
before the old Bill puts the handcuffs on your
dear old dad and slings him in jail. Get the
picture?'

'What about Mum?' asked Lester.

189

'I think the old girl's done a runner,' said Ricky.

'Just like Sid,' said Lester gloomily.

Ricky Sparks smiled, flashing his gold tooth. 'As always, son, I am a man with a plan.'

27
Wilted

Mindy had spent the night over at Lucy's. There was no mystery as to who had taken Ernest. Tom had seen Lester run off with the shoebox and then there was the dropped lollipop, as if any more proof was needed. Lucy had been all for going over to Sparks's Garden Centre and demanding him back. Dad had said that would be unwise and if she would just wait he would go round there in the morning. Still, that had been of little comfort to Lucy.

That night, while Ricky Sparks had been in the grip of a Venus Flytrap, his wife had been up in the belfry and Miss Robinson had been hiding behind a filing cabinet.

All Lucy had been able to do was toss and turn. It wasn't until the birds had started to sing that finally she dropped off to sleep.

The dawning of the wedding day was not a peaceful one. Conrad, too, had been up most of the night. There was so much to do before a big wedding like this. Little things just seemed to pile up. And there had been all that fuss over the security guard's uniform that had gone missing.

But it wasn't until seven in the morning that the disaster was discovered. Someone had broken in and turned the heating in the marquee on full blast, so that all the flowers had wilted. Conrad phoned Mr Willow.

'Sabotage!' shrieked Conrad hysterically. 'The roses have wilted, the arbour is ruined!'

'What?' said Dad, bleary-eyed, groping for the alarm clock.

'My career is over! I'm finished! I'm nothing more than dried-up rose petals on the church steps!' wailed Conrad.

'Don't panic,' said Dad, panicking. 'I'll be there.'

Dad picked up Stench who was gurgling in his cot and went to wake Lucy.

'Conrad's just phoned,' said Dad. 'Someone's been tampering with the flowers and they've all wilted. You've got to help. We need your magic fingers. Get up, Socks.' And he went off to phone Miss Fortwell.

Mindy too woke up. 'What's happened?' she asked.

'I don't know,' said Lucy. 'It's the flowers. They've wilted. Dad needs my help.' A sudden awful thought struck her. 'Oh no! How can I help without Ernest? Without him my fingers just won't tingle, I know they won't.'

'I'm sure your dad will get Ernest back,' said Mindy.

'But I need him now!' said Lucy. 'What shall I do?'

Before Mindy could reply, a horn sounded outside.

'Come on, you three,' said Miss Fortwell. 'We haven't a moment to lose.'

Mum came to the carriage door with Stench. 'Good luck!' she shouted.

They arrived at Silverboots' mansion to be greeted by Conrad who looked the colour of over-worked clay; grey.

'If Blossom B finds out this will ruin her day, ruin it. I tell you, it's like the Sahara in there. It's all over bar the shouting.' He was almost weeping.

They all followed him into the marquee.

'Look at this,' said Conrad.

It was a most alarming sight. All the flowers hung their heads. Some had just wilted in the heat, others looked dried up.

'I suggest you go up to the house and make yourself a good strong cup of tea,' said Miss Fortwell. 'Now, if you could give us some space, Lucy has some work to do.'

'Please just do some magic, please, anything, I beg you,' said Conrad.

'It's a disaster,' said Dad after he had gone. 'Lucy, you'd better get going.'

'I can't,' said Lucy. 'I haven't got Ernest. We're a team.'

'No,' said Dad. 'No, not now. Look, I said I would get Ernest back and I will, but baby, Socks, Socks, this is an emergency. This needs your — '

'I'm really sorry, Dad, but I know the Sparkses will never give Ernest back. They'll just say they haven't got him. Anyway, by now he could be just a crushed shell,' said Lucy. Hot and angry tears rolled down her face. 'I just can't do it without — '

Miss Fortwell coughed.

'I think, George,' she said firmly, 'that you should go and help Conrad with the tea. Now, leave me your mobile and go.'

Once they were alone, she went on, 'Lucy, I

need to ask you some very important questions. Did Ernest ever come out of his  shoebox when you were doing the tingling thing with your fingers?'

'No,' said Lucy, 'but without him my fingers just don't tingle.'

'Did they ever tingle when Ernest wasn't with you?'

'No. Oh yes, actually, once,' said Lucy, 'when Bert asked me to stick my fingers in some baby sweet peas and he said he would tell me if it was me or my snail that made things grow.'

'And did he?' asked Miss Fortwell.

'He went away on holiday and I never saw him again to ask,' said Lucy.

'Hold it right there,' said Miss Fortwell. She phoned the hospital. 'Ward three, please. I want to speak to Mr Mudd.'

Lucy sat miserably under the arbour, looking at all the wilted roses.

'Will you tell Lucy that?' said Miss Fortwell, passing Lucy the phone.

'They did,' said Lucy, repeating every word Mr Mudd was saying, 'and you took them home because you had never seen anything like it!'

Lucy handed the phone back to Miss Fortwell, who thanked Mr Mudd and told him he had saved the day.

'I don't understand,' said Mr Mudd. 'What's going on?'

'Tell you later, old thing,' said Miss Fortwell, switching off the mobile. She sat down next to Lucy.

'Are you ready for a little lesson on snails and gardening?'

Then she told Lucy in no uncertain terms what snails do, and how they are not, as she might suppose, gardeners' friends and how garden centres have shelves dedicated to killing them.

'So you don't think Ernest had anything to do with my green fingers,' said Lucy.

'Nothing,' said Miss Fortwell.

'But Ernest was a king amongst snails.'

'Then don't let him down,' said Miss

Fortwell. 'What would he say if he was with you?'

Lucy looked at Miss Fortwell and threw her arms around her. 'You're right. He would think I was being pants.'

'And that doesn't sound good?' said Miss Fortwell, who had no idea what was meant by pants.

'It's being silly and soppy.'

'All things that one isn't,' said Miss Fortwell.

All of a sudden Lucy was wide awake and her fingers began to tingle in a delicious kind of way. She looked again at all the wilting and drooping flowers.

'This isn't the same as sticking your fingers in the earth like when they were seedlings, is it?' said Lucy.

'No,' said Miss Fortwell. 'I think you should just chat to them and explain how much they are needed. That sort of thing. Remember how vain flowers are. They do like to look their best, especially at weddings. Would you like me to leave you alone while you do that?'

'No,' said Lucy. She stood for a minute in the

middle of the marquee, her hands out before
her, her eyes closed. Then she opened them
and went round all the flowers, talking to them
and gently cupping them in her hands. Miss
Fortwell hardly dared breathe. She watched in
awe as each and every flower came back to life,
as if waking from an enchanted sleep.

28
The Wedding of the Century

'It's nothing short of magic,'
wept Conrad when at last he
was allowed back into the
marquee. 'You are the child
wonder of the flower world.'

'I'm glad you're pleased,'
said Lucy, smiling as she stood there amongst
the revived flowers that all seemed a little
larger and more beautiful than before.

'I am thunderstruck by your brilliance! I
shall be using Peppercorn Plants for every
major wedding I do, and that is a promise.'

Dad felt almost giddy with pride as he walked
towards the car with Lucy, Mindy and Miss
Fortwell. 'You are a star, no, more than a star,
you are the best daughter anyone can have.'

'Wait!' Conrad shouted. 'Don't go. Any of
you.'

'Oh no,' said Dad, his heart sinking into his boots. 'What now?'

Conrad caught them up, quite out of breath. 'You've got to come up to the house. Blossom B wants to see you.'

'Is everything all right?' asked Dad nervously as they stood in the hall. Blossom B came down the stairs towards them, her hair in rollers.

'No, it blooming well ain't,' said Blossom B.

'Is it the flowers?' said Dad shakily.

'No, it ain't the blooming flowers. They're picture perfect. The problem is my bridesmaid. I've only got one, haven't I, Tallulah's daughter Posy. She's just gone and got blooming chickenpox, hasn't she.'

'Wow,' said Lucy. 'Is that Tallulah the supermodel?'

'That's right, my best mate. Now I'm in a right pickle.'

'Oh dear,' said Dad. 'I don't know how we can help.'

'I'll tell you how you can help, Mr Willow. You've got a very pretty daughter with the greenest fingers in the country.' She smiled at

Lucy. 'I'd be right chuffed if you would be my bridesmaid.'

'Wow!' said Lucy, jumping up and down with excitement. 'I've never ever been a bridesmaid. Oh gazoo, how exciting!'

'And as for you guys,' said Blossom B, looking at Dad, Mindy and Miss Fortwell, 'better go home and get your glad rags on. I want you to be at my wedding. Bring Tom if he wants to come, and don't forget Mrs Willow and Zac.'

Lucy almost floated as she went up the stairs with Blossom B. Her hair and makeup were

done by an artist. Her green fingers even had a manicure. Gosh, thought Lucy, I could get used to this life.

The dress had been made for Posy, but it was just the right length for Lucy. She had never seen such a glamorous dress, let alone worn one. It had real pearls sewn on it, and as for the shoes, Cinderella would have been proud of them. With all the fuss that was made of her, Lucy felt like a princess.

Sometimes things work out in the most unexpected ways. Who would have thought that having magic fingers would have led Lucy to this moment?

'Think it's all right then?' asked Blossom B as she and Lucy were driven to the church in the silver Bentley.

'It's more than all right. You look like a fairy queen,' said Lucy.

'And you must be the princess of the flowers,' said Blossom B. 'Are you nervous?'

'A bit,' said Lucy.

'So am I,' giggled Blossom B.

Crowds lined the route and cameras flashed and a band played as they drove up to the church, where more cameras clicked and popped.

'Good luck!' shouted some of the onlookers.

'You're a lucky girl!' shouted others.

The organ sang out 'Here comes the bride,' and Lucy walked behind Blossom B into the church, holding her train. She could see Mum and Dad and Stench sitting there as well as Mindy and Tom, who looked goggle-eyed to see the whole of the England football team.

The church was full of the flowers Lucy had helped grow. She followed Blossom B up the aisle to the arbour of pink and white roses where Silverboots McCoy, the handsomest man in the world, was waiting.

Afterwards, more photos were taken on the steps of the church. Then the wedding party all got back into their cars and drove up to the mansion for the reception in the marquee.

After they had gone the church fell silent. The vicar was changing in the vestry when he heard a muffled cry. He went out into the church and stood there listening. In the silence that followed a dull scream could be heard. For a moment the vicar wondered if there was a

ghost in the belfry. He called up,
'Hello, is anyone there?' and a
Gucci slipper fell at his feet.

29

Comeuppance

The day of the wedding was the day the Sparkses got their comeuppance. Petunia Sparks was arrested inside the church for misusing school funds and for keeping stolen property on the school premises. Later several other charges were brought, not least that of stealing the money for the church bells.

'I've done nothing wrong. Do you know who I am?' shouted Mrs Sparks when they brought her to the police station, still wearing her dressing-gown, her hair sticking up from having hung upside down for so long. 'I am Petunia Sparks, head teacher of Maldon — '

She stopped. Sitting on a chair was Miss Robinson. 'What are you doing here?'

'I am here as a witness to a crime,' said Miss Robinson, standing up.

'What crime, you idiot woman?' snapped Mrs Sparks. Just at that moment Stan was brought in.

'What are you doing here, Stan?' said Mrs Sparks without thinking.

'You know each other, then,' asked the detective.

Mrs Sparks knew there was nowhere to run. 'I want to see my lawyer,' she shouted as she was taken to the cells.

'This way, Miss Robinson,' said a policeman kindly. 'Sorry to keep you waiting. If you don't mind we would like to take a statement.'

What Miss Robinson had to say was enough to have Petunia Sparks put behind bars for a very long time indeed. It appeared that she was better known to Fat Harry's mob as Sapphire Slim, the leader of the gang. She had forged all her qualifications. She had never taken an exam in her life and never been to Oxford. She had used all the school funds on shopping for clothes, hairdos, shoes, and holidays in Spain. That was not all. She had been using the school to take in and receive stolen goods.

On the night Miss Robinson had gone to the school, Stan was there to make the last pick-up. He was surprised, he said in court, that the boss wasn't there.

'By boss,' said Stan's lawyer, 'you mean Ricky Sparks.'

'No,' said Stan. 'He couldn't organise his way out of a brown paper bag. No, I mean Sapphire Slim. She's the boss.'

To give Mrs Sparks her due, she never said that Ricky was involved. She never said she was guilty, either. The jury, though, had no doubt that Mrs Sparks was a bad penny, and she was sent to Holloway women's prison.

Now you might well be wondering what became of Ricky Sparks and his son Lester, the chip off the old block. They both made their escape and left England's green and pleasant land for the sunnier shores of Spain, where Ricky opened a pub, which was much more up his street. Lester too, soon got used to life in Spain. Occasionally he remembered to send his mum a card.

A few days after the wedding, while Mrs Sparks was awaiting trial, even more charges were brought against her. It had now been proved that the will giving Pip Peppercorn's business to the Sparkses was a forgery. The true last will and testament had been found by Miss Robinson in the head teacher's desk, along with all the notes on the rose that the Peppercorns had been trying to grow.

When Bert and Betty Peppercorn returned home, it took them a bit of time to take in all that had happened. There was a lot to take in.

Sparks's Garden Centre now belonged to Bert Peppercorn and the order books were already full. Dad had given away the stocks of fish and reptiles to specialist centres. Peppercorn's, said Bert, were going to concentrate on good old-fashioned plants.

Bert wasted no time getting back to Sparks's Garden Centre. Carefully he lifted up the floorboards in the office Ricky had used. Little did Mr Sparks know that he had been sitting on a goldmine. There were the rosebushes all carefully wrapped up waiting to be potted. And with a little help from Lucy's green fingers, the Peppercorns' dream could be realised at last.

That evening Mum cooked a very special dinner for everyone. Dad put up trestle tables alongside the train, and Miss Fortwell brought along a gramophone with a huge horn that played very silly records that made Lucy laugh.

'Remember those sweet peas?' said Bert. 'That's what I was trying to tell you before I left, except it went clean out of my head. I was so impressed, I gave them to Mr Mudd to keep an eye on. I hope he got a chance to tell you about them.'

After Mum had brought out the strawberries and cream Bert tapped his glass and stood up.

'Well, this is what Betty and me want to say. We want to thank you, more than thank you, for restoring my business to me, and for doing a wonderful job at the wedding. So Betty and me would like to show our gratitude, and this is how. First, this splendid home of yours has no land to call its own, so to speak. We would like you to put your carriages up at the old garden centre, and we would also like you, George, to be a partner in Peppercorn Enterprises.'

The Willow family let out a huge cheer. 'Thank you, thank you,' said Mum.

'Wait, that's not all. I want you to be the first to know that the new rose, grown with Lucy's help, will be called LUCY WILLOW.'

Just then Stench, who had just started crawling, called out 'errshnail!' Lucy looked to see that her little brother had a snail in his tiny fingers. Not just any snail. He had Ernest.

'Oh well done, Zac,' said Lucy, feeling for the first time that there was quite a lot to be said for having a baby brother. And thinking about it, the name Stench didn't suit him at all.

'Pretty clever to find Ernest, don't you think?' she said to Mum.

'Yes.' Mum paused. Then she said, smiling, 'Stench is a good brother to have.'

'Oh, Mum,' said Lucy firmly, 'his name is Zac, for pity's sake.'

Which made both of them start to giggle.

So that's all I have to tell you about Lucy Willow, who had a snail for a pet and lived on a train. People often asked the new head teacher, Miss Robinson, how the sunflowers got so big, but she always said that perhaps it was something in the soil. Who would believe her if she told the truth?

For after all Lucy Willow is only eight, and with such a magical gift can you imagine what more she could do when she gets older?